Mark turned ofed
it back to Jade, tryin   ut
clearly annoyed, loc   w
territorial some of t   n
stations can be. Th   er
weather jockey atte _____ .... on a
patch of grass or beach.

"The Mali Kai manager already gave us clearance
to stay here for the duration of the storm. He assured
my producer that we would get exclusive use of the
grounds."

Mark shrugged. "Well, my producer wanted us
here, too, so I'm not sure what to say." He extended a
hand. "Mark Fox. Bay News 9."

"I know who you are," the woman spat back. "You
don't remember me, do you?"

Mark narrowed his eyes and struggled to recollect
if he knew the indignant woman standing before him
getting soaked in the declining weather. Deep-set, light
brown eyes, thick, wavy hair, and full lips all framed by
a heart-shaped face gave the woman a distinctive and
undeniably attractive look. Despite her pretty features,
Mark drew a blank, and the more time he spent staring
down this angry woman in the rain, the more he wished
he could remember if he actually knew her or not.
"Can't say I recall. Should I?"

"USF Journalism program?" She exhaled deeply.

Even in the dim light of a stormy, early evening,
Mark detected a hint of red on her cheeks. Her eyes
glinted and shone with the same rage he recognized
before in the face of so many jilted ex-lovers.

Weathering Heights

by

Wendy Dalrymple

Weathering Heights

Cover Art by *Diana Carlile*

The Wild Rose Press, Inc.
PO Box 708
Adams Basin, NY 14410-0708
Visit us at www.thewildrosepress.com

Publishing History
First Edition, 2023
Trade Paperback ISBN 978-1-5092-4697-7
Digital ISBN 978-1-5092-4698-4

Published in the United States of America

Chapter One

Melody Orlean stared out the rain-spattered window of the WINK News van into the oncoming storm overhead and wrinkled her nose. Stormy US 41 sped by in a blur of swaying palm trees outside, while dark, ominous clouds blotted out the normally bright, southwest Florida sun. An offensive aroma permeated the air of the cramped work van and punched her right in the nostrils, stinging her eyes. Her driver and cameraman, Ty, focused on the road as he navigated through the weather with one hand on the wheel and the other gripping a meatless fast-food burger loaded with onions. The sound of him crunching and chewing was only blotted out by the wind and patter of rain, for which Melody was grateful.

"Couldn't you have waited until we got to the Mali Kai?" Melody shifted in her seat and found her purse, mumbling as she searched for the beat-up tote bag she used for work. Her makeup organizer contained heavy-duty on-air essentials: ibuprofen, wet wipes, mace, a toothbrush, and all of the personal items she would need for a weekend on assignment. She glanced in the visor mirror to see if her waterproof mascara needed a touch-up or if anything was stuck in her teeth, but thankfully, everything was still in place. Melody's matte fuchsia lip color offset her tawny complexion and bobbed mass of thick and wavy dark hair, all of which was also still in perfect condition. Her black, chiffon ruffled blouse and pencil skirt, on the other hand, were in danger of being soiled by Ty's lunch. But as long as she didn't get fast-food grease anywhere on her person, Melody would be sure to remain camera-ready when they arrived at their location.

"Babe, I don't eat meat, and I have been *dying* for a fast-food burger," Ty said. "South Fort Myers is the only place I can find them right now."

"Yeah, but you could have waited until we got into the resort," she teased. Melody closed the mirrored visor. "Now I'm going to smell like ketchup and meatless mystery meat."

"Oh, *please*." Ty rolled his eyes. "You know just as well as I do that hurricanes are unpredictable. I wouldn't want to take the chance of missing something because I waited to eat. Plus my dinner would have gotten cold."

"You're right. Sorry, I'm cranky. I haven't eaten anything healthy all day."

"Plant-based diet, baby. I swear by it. Good for the planet. Good for you, too." Ty took another bite of his sandwich and kept his focus on the rainy, windswept highway. Her coworker, cameraman, and driver certainly looked the part of someone who took care of himself—from his perfect deep complexion right down to his trim physique. Ty also seemed to be in a perpetually cheerful mood, something that both baffled and endeared him to her all at once.

Melody tried her best to cheer up despite her building anxiety, resisting the urge to pick her manicure. She let out a deep, stress-relieving sigh and rolled down the window ever so slightly, then rolled it up again as rainwater poured in. "This storm is picking up faster than all of the spaghetti models forecast. Global warming is a hoax…yeah, right."

Ty snort-laughed. "Maybe if they called the storm forecast graphs something other than *spaghetti models,* people would listen."

"I guess. This tropical storm is nothing compared to what we'll see once Hurricane Lorraine moves in. The flooding is gonna be *bad*, no two ways about it. I'm really worried for the people who refuse to leave."

"Well, that's why we're risking our necks, right?" Ty said. "So we can show folks this storm is no joke."

"I wish there was more that I could do, though. It's not safe for anyone to be in the middle of a major storm, even us, and *especially* at some rickety old hotel."

Ty slowed the van to a swaying stop light as a wall of rain came down. "Listen. I know you're worried about staying at the Mali Kai, but I think it'll be fun. Hurricanes are always exciting, but it's even better when you have a tiki bar at your disposal."

Melody gave him a side-eyed look and smiled. "It's weird that Anthony insisted we station there for this storm, right? All the alcohol in the world won't help when we're knee-deep in water."

The Mali Kai resort at Fort Myers Beach was ancient and tacky, even back when Melody and her girlfriends used to party there in high school. She could only imagine how bad it must be now. Melody could almost smell the saltwater must of the carpet, the ozone air conditioner, and the stale cigarette smoke that lingered in the curtains. Mali Kai used the term "resort" liberally.

"I actually used to hang out at the Mali Kai as a teen," she snorted. "Must be practically crumbling by now."

"Well, they have hurricane-grade windows." Ty chuckled, shaking his head. "Anthony called to make sure. He's always worried about liability. Like you can even try to anticipate what will happen in a storm."

"I guess if worse comes to worst, we can order their Mai Tai bucket and enjoy the storm from behind a solid inch of safety glass." She shrugged, her shoulders easing a bit.

"This your first hurricane?" he asked.

Melody shook her head. "I've experienced my fair share. I've been working out of Florida for a while, but after college, I covered Hurricane Charlie and Wilma for the *Sarasota Sun*." Melody stared up at the fast moving clouds overhead. "I've lived through a few hurricanes, actually. I grew up around here and saw some of the worst."

"Oh yeah? My boyfriend grew up here too, but not me. I'm from Kansas."

"Ah, so you know all about tornados then." Melody nodded.

"Yup. I would take a thousand hurricanes before one tornado. Talk about unpredictable."

"That reminds me." Melody searched for her phone. "I need to text my brother Austin and make sure my mom is doing okay. Hurricanes freak her out." Melody shot off a quick text message as the news van bumped along, the rain tapped in hard, heavy droplets on the roof. She frowned and stared out the window toward the rows and rows of coral and turquoise buildings that lined the causeway as her

4

cameraman/driver grew silent.

She still didn't know Ty or anyone else at the station very well, but so far, her only other coworker on the road seemed to be an okay guy. She would need a friend for this long and stormy weekend; it was Melody's second shift as WINK's new junior weekend meteorologist which coincided with the landfall of Hurricane Lorraine, the biggest, most hyped-up storm the Gulf Coast saw in some thirty years.

"Are we almost there?" Melody yawned. "I have to pee before we do our establishing shot."

"Yep, just another mile or two." Ty craned his neck to see through the steady drizzle of rain.

After a few more minutes of bumping along the causeway, Ty's chewing finally stopped, and the Mali Kai at Fort Myers Beach came into view. The looming, rectangular beach resort wasn't anything special and looked like every other big-box hotel on the beach built in the 1960s. The only difference was the Mali Kai distinguished itself from the Sandpiper and the Windstar and the Pink Shell with its kitschy pseudo-Polynesian aesthetic. While Melody used to enjoy visiting the landmark resort long ago, now as an adult she looked on the place with disdain at its half-hearted attempt at cultural appropriation.

"What in the…?" Ty pulled the news van under the hotel reception overhang offering a little relief from the rain.

Melody rolled down her window as her eyes narrowed in the overcast light. In the distance, just off the side of the parking lot, idled a Bay News 9 *Weather on the Nines!* news truck that most certainly should *not* have been there. Melody pursed her lips and took in the grayish-green waters of the Gulf of Mexico as they churned and frothed in the distance while an ominous, dark sky accumulated overhead. Most alarming was the pixie-ish videographer and meteorologist who were already hard at work. He was a tall, blond mannequin of a man in a blue poncho with his body hunched over as he braced himself against the not-so-windy wind in an overly dramatic fashion.

Mark Fox.

Melody emerged from the news van, and her expensive veneers gnashed together. She was already battling a tension headache from earlier that day, and now her jaw ached along with the pulsing pain at her temples. The wind whipped at her hair, ruining her earlier efforts to appear camera-ready. A lash of rain smacked her on the cheek, but she hardly took notice.

"They're not supposed to be here." Ty leaned up against the news van and mirrored Melody's cross-armed stance.

"Yeah, no *kidding.*" Melody huffed, regarding the ridiculous scene. She didn't know how or why Bay News 9's star meteorologist decided to edge in on *her* territory when the entire Gulf Coast would be pummeled in the next twenty-four hours. Mark and his crew from Tampa could have their pick of prime locations. Why did they have to pick the one filming spot she and her producer squared away as their own?

"I wonder if they have clearance from the manager to film here, too." Ty opened the back doors of the van and propped his hands on his hips.

"I don't know." Melody rubbed her temples and forced her teeth to unclamp. "But I'll find out."

Chapter Two

Mark Fox readjusted the hood of his slicker and leaned ever so slightly against the wind as droplets of rain stung at his face. The Gulf of Mexico raged behind him—a dark, roiling sea of warm, murky green hissed as the wind whipped at its shores. Only a few hours before, Mark decided to race to Fort Myers in the middle of a tropical storm to be the first meteorologist on air to break the dramatic change of direction Hurricane Lorraine took. As a result, he didn't have time to change into his usual hurricane reporting gear. Mark glanced at his feet and frowned; his new Italian leather loafers were already ruined.

"Jade, how's the shot?" he called over the building storm.

"You look great," the videographer yelled back. Jade gave a thumbs-up from behind a black boxy camera shrouded in its own rain cover. The wind whistled at his back, signaling the storm was picking up momentum. Mark needed to get the most dramatic shots possible to keep his viewers engaged, and the conditions were right. He didn't like how dramatized some of his weather reports turned out, but it was what his producers and his fans wanted, and ratings were king.

"Lean forward a bit more. Really emphasize the atmosphere!"

"Oh. Okay!" Mark's eyes widened, and his lips pulled back into a megawatt smile.

"Ready?"

Mark nodded and braced his body into a hunched position.

"Five. Four." Jade shouted. She mouthed the remainder of the countdown and pointed in Mark's direction at number one.

"We're out here at the Mali Kai Resort at Fort Myers Beach, and boy, things are really picking up," Mark shouted into his mic, still leaning into the wind in a dramatic fashion. "We just got word that the beaches are being evacuated within the hour, and local law enforcement is encouraging all residents to get out while they still can."

Mark held a hand to his ear, listening for his cue from Teri Nightingale back in the studio in Tampa. This was his one shining moment during the six o'clock news, and he didn't want to disappoint his fans. He shot a huge, cheesy grin into the camera as he waited for Jade to give him the thumbs-up. Then he could chime back the signature sign-off he used for over a decade at Bay News 9.

"Check back in with you all later! In Fort Myers Beach, I'm Mark Fox." Mark waited for Jade to give the all-clear and resumed his normal posture. He lifted a foot and was met with a wet, gulping sound as the beach sucked at his ruined new shoes.

"I gotta remember to pack sandals next time," he yelled to Jade. As he flung chunks of sand from his shoes, a voice cut through the storm that most certainly didn't belong to his videographer.

"Just what do you think you're doing?"

Mark looked up from his soaked leather loafers and squinted against the falling rain. A visibly angry woman in a red poncho and shiny black rain boots marched toward him; her pencil skirt, blouse, and entire ensemble were shrouded beneath a much nicer, see-through rain barrier than the one he borrowed from Jade. Between the WINK News van in the distance and the very specific style of hair and makeup this woman wore, Mark suspected this upset woman must be with the press, too.

"I'm doing the six o'clock news. What's it look like?" Mark turned off his weatherproof mic and handed it back to Jade, trying hard not to look at the pretty, but clearly annoyed local reporter. He was aware of how territorial some of the journalists from the small town stations can be. This wasn't the first time another weather jockey attempted to stake their claim on a patch of grass or beach.

"The Mali Kai manager already gave us clearance to stay here for the duration of the storm. He assured my producer that we would get *exclusive* use of the grounds."

Mark shrugged. "Well my producer wanted us here, too, so I'm not sure what to say." He extended a hand. "Mark Fox. Bay News 9."

"I know who you *are*," the woman spat back. "You don't remember me, do you?"

Mark narrowed his eyes and struggled to recollect if he knew the indignant woman standing before him getting soaked in the declining weather. Deep-set, light brown eyes, thick, wavy hair, and full lips all framed by a heart-shaped face gave the woman a distinctive and undeniably attractive look. Despite her pretty features,

Mark drew a blank, and the more time he spent staring down this angry woman in the rain, the more he wished he could remember if he actually knew her or not. "Can't say I recall. Should I?"

"USF journalism program?" She exhaled deeply.

Even in the dim light of a stormy, early evening, Mark could detect a hint of red on her cheeks. Her eyes glinted and shone with the same rage he'd recognized before in the face of so many jilted ex-lovers. Boy did he ever wish he could remember who she was.

"Melody Orlean. We went to college together for *four years*!" Her hands flew in the air.

Mark shook his head and frowned. He struggled to recollect, and a twinge of embarrassment crept up his spine. College hadn't exactly been the high point of his life, and he squeaked by to get his degree as it was. Many details from that time in his life he didn't remember, a point he wasn't particularly proud of.

"I'm sorry, I really don't remember." He glanced up at the very heavy and very low hanging clouds overhead. "Can we take this inside? I need to get some rest and prepare for the eleven o'clock."

"Wait, are you *staying* here?"

The woman stomped toward the resort, causing her boots to splash through the puddles of accumulated rain in a dramatic, child-like fashion.

Jade made a face and shrugged. She followed at his heels and toted her camera through the storm.

A tall man leaned against the WINK News van with his arms crossed at his chest and a grin spread across his lips. He waved at Jade.

"We're set up in the first-floor executive conference room," Mark called over his shoulder. "The managers have blocked off all of the hotel rooms for now since they are evacuating."

Even through the storm, Mark could still hear the woman become audibly frustrated with him from behind.

She sucked in a deep, ragged breath through her nose. "We'll see about that," she mumbled. Melody huffed one last time and sped past Mark and Jade toward the local news van in a blur of red poncho and dark hair.

Mark shook his head and continued through the vestibule entrance of the Mali Kai as the sky rumbled in the background.

A stampede of hotel guests made a flurried exit, pushing their way out of the hotel in droves.

Mark felt bad for them; they were probably regular people from Ohio or Minnesota or Canada enjoying their late summer vacation. They were right to be afraid though. From the forecasts and models Mark studied on the way down from Tampa, Hurricane Lorraine looked like it was far worse than everyone originally feared.

"What was that all about?" Jade glanced over her shoulder at the parked news van. "Have you got old history with Ty's meteorologist or something?"

Mark turned his attention to the direction of the hotel overhang. The woman—Melody, she said her name was—waved her arms in the air and argued with the man Jade called Ty. He let out a deep sigh. "I don't know. They said that they got clearance to be here first. You know how local news people can be."

"I can talk to Ty if you want?" Jade said. "We took videography classes at Full Sail together. He's a good guy."

"I don't think that's necessary." Mark breezed through the hallway of the Mali Kai past potted faux palm trees and tiki statues. "They'll either give us our space or move on."

He pushed the double doors to the hotel conference room open and entered their makeshift stakeout for the next twenty-four to forty-eight hours. He kicked off his soaked and now *ruined* expensive loafers and sank into the rolling cot the hotel set up, eager for a much-needed nap. His back was still aching from the long drive from Tampa, and now he was cold and wet to boot, but the cot was about as good as it would get. He slowed his breathing and settled in. Still, the furious local reporter continued to dance through his mind, her angry eyes flashing and her pretty lips pressed together in a thin, hate-filled line.

Melody Orlean.

Maybe he *had* heard the name before, but he couldn't honestly say. As the hurried footsteps of evacuating hotel guests continued to thunder outside his door, the wind and rain picked up outside. The storm wasn't on its way to Fort Myers Beach; it was already here. With his mind and body still buzzing, Mark pulled out his phone to investigate and research the woman who was staking a claim at the Mali Kai. Maybe he didn't know who she was right away, but now as a loud boom of thunder rumbled overhead, Mark decided to find out for sure.

Chapter Three

"My producer Anthony *assured* me we would have *exclusive* use of the resort." Melody tapped her foot at the harried woman behind the guest services counter. A buzz of frantic resort guests shuffled behind her and Ty in a wave. They spilled into the vestibule and loaded into rental cars with suitcases and overnight bags at hand.

Ty leaned against the counter backward resting on his elbows, taking in the hectic scene with a smirk.

Melody tried to exude a sense of patience and calm as she reasoned with the resort employee again.

"Ma'am, our manager is currently out of the country, and he didn't leave any notes about this." The disinterested receptionist clicked her mouse. "The only information we have is to make sure everyone evacuates the resort except for essential workers."

Ma'am. Mental sirens fired and a wave of red flooded Melody's vision. Her current situation went from bad to worse, and the indifferent resort employee wasn't helping. However, as someone who worked in the service industry in the past, Melody knew the guest services clerk wasn't at fault. She closed her eyes and readjusted her attitude toward the hotel employee.

"Okay." She forced a smile. "Where do we stay then?"

The woman looked up from her work and pointed a

glittery, gel manicured fingernail past them and down the hall. "Where all of the other press has to stay. In the conference room."

Melody turned her head and stared down the hallway crowded with scrambling resort guests. The same hallway where the Bay News 9 crew retreated to only moments before. She clenched her jaw and turned back to the receptionist.

"No. No, no, no, no, no. That's not acceptable. Ty, let's go." Melody spun around, certain if she were in a cartoon, steam would be shooting from her ears. How could this happen? The biggest storm of the year, possibly of the decade, was on a direct path to the Mali Kai and not only was she being forced to share a filming location but a *room* with Mark Fox. Absolutely *not*.

"It's cool, Mel. We can just go film at the Sandpiper." Ty followed to the empty hotel lounge.

Melody flopped onto a rattan chair, her face still burning as she pulled out her work phone. Her hands shook as she smashed the buttons on the glass screen to call her producer.

"No. I'll get Anthony to fix this. If he's going to send us out in the middle of a tropical storm right before a Cat 3...dangit!" Melody listened as Anthony's phone went straight to voicemail. She ended the call with a flourish, then punched out a carefully chosen text message requesting him to call her back *immediately*. "Well, he didn't pick up, and we can't move a muscle without clearance." She tapped her feet and waited a moment before dialing her producer again. She listened but only got the same automated message.

"What about Julie?" Ty offered. "Want me to give

her a call?"

Melody shook her head. "Julie started having contractions this morning. She's having a *baby* in the middle of all this. She's got more to worry about right now than which hotel we're staying at."

"Oooh, that's rough." Ty winced.

Melody and Ty stared out the back window of the Mali Kai lounge at the pool deck overlooking the tiki bar and a vacant stretch of Fort Myers Beach. Only twelve hours ago, all of Lee County was bracing for Tropical Storm Paul, a small system with sustained winds of sixty miles per hour. Everyone, including Melody, let down their guard when it came to the other huge system accumulating in the Atlantic Ocean at the same time off the coast of Africa. Slowly but surely, the unassuming storm organized and was expected to pass over the Caribbean as a Category 1 or 2 hurricane at most, eventually becoming Hurricane Lorraine. A combination of warm gulf temperatures and low pressure systems unexpectedly pushed the hurricane onto a new course following the coattails of Tropical Storm Paul. Fort Myers Beach was about to get directly hit by back-to-back storms.

The puffy charcoal clouds hanging low over the Gulf of Mexico flew by faster than ever as the last sliver of light faded from the sky. Even though it rained on and off, Melody already knew the storm was about to ramp up dramatically. They were running out of time to set up an establishing shot and stake out a filming location. If they had to hop to another hotel, they needed to do it *fast*.

"Should I just go unload the gear in the conference room?" Ty asked, his brow furrowed. "It won't be so bad to stick it out here, I promise. I know Jade, and she's cool."

"Ughh, that's not the point!" Melody huffed. "I know I must sound like an absolute brat right now, but you have no idea what kind of *hell* Mark Fox put me through."

Ty snort-laughed through his nose. "Okay, he does kind of look like he might be full of himself, but believe me, you've got nothing to worry about. You're better than that guy."

Melody exhaled a slow, controlled breath through her nose and glanced up at her cameraman through a heavy coating of mascara. Ty was proving himself to be nice and easygoing and all she could do was act like a prima donna. She couldn't in good conscience put him out and make him run all over Fort Myers Beach in the middle of a storm because of a clerical error. "Fine." She sighed. "I'll suck it up, I guess. We need to get to work anyway."

"I'll go back and talk to the lady at guest services and tell her we need to get set up." Ty rose from his chair. "I don't think she likes you too much."

"Well, she can join the club." Melody frowned and buried her face in her hands. "I don't like myself so much right now either."

Ty gave her shoulder a squeeze and took off back toward the customer service desk to officially check them in.

Melody continued to monitor the storm outside and also tried to quell the storm that was brewing inside of her, too. Having to share accommodations with any other meteorology crew during a hurricane wasn't ideal, but being in close quarters with someone she so obviously loathed would prove to be a challenge.

It's just for a couple of days. Can it really be that bad?

****

Melody and Ty followed two burly resort employees to the common area space with their necessities at hand. With a loud bang, the rolling cots skidded into the far wall of the resort conference room, sending a grinding, metallic thud into the air. Melody could barely contain her glee when Mark Fox yelped and bolted upright in his cot.

"Ah!"

"Hey, sorry, man." Ty held up a hand in his direction. "They're sticking us in here with you."

Mark grumbled, turned over in his cot, and buried his head under a pillow. "Can you keep it down?"

"No biggie." Jade slapped Ty a high five. "There's plenty of room here. It'll be nice to have some company, too."

Melody frowned at the sleeping lump that was Mark Fox, then turned her attention back to the two hulks who wheeled in their foldout cots. The cutest of the two resort security guards handed Melody a stack of linens and a pillow and grinned like the cat who ate the canary. She flicked her gaze to his plastic name tag. "So, Russel...do you happen to know where I can freshen up?"

"There's a bathroom in the hall next to the vending machines." The security guard ran his thumb and index finger along his jawline. "There won't be any room service during the storm though, just FYI."

"That's okay. I think we'll make do." She forced a smile. The urge to pee was greater than ever now.

Melody wouldn't be able to cross her legs for much longer.

"What news channel are you with?"

Russel continued to practically undress her with his eyes as she inched toward the door.

Ty and Jade chatted in the opposite corner of the room, oblivious while Mark continued to nap.

"WINK." An icky sensation crept into her gut. "Thank you so much for all your help, I'm just going to excuse myself."

"I'll be here in the security station through the storm." Russel licked his lips. "If you, uh, need to take a shower or anything, I can show you where the employee bathrooms are."

Melody suppressed the urge to cringe. "That won't be necessary."

Russel and his coworker lingered in the conference room cracking jokes with Ty.

Melody hurried into the hall in search of the bathroom, eager to get away from his leering eyes. She was relieved to finally have a moment of peace before the next forty-eight hours of stress she was headed into, and she could use a nice private bathroom panic attack session. Once she figured out how the lock worked on the bamboo bathroom door, Melody readjusted her hair and makeup again and ignored her growling stomach and racing thoughts.

Food. That lunkhead said, there was a vending machine in the hall, right?

At that moment, Melody wished she ordered a meatless burger, too, when she had the chance. She and Ty were scheduled to film their opening shot for the eight o'clock news, so something fast would be in order to ease her appetite. In her haste to leave her apartment that afternoon, she forgot her lunch box filled with all of her "healthy" storm snacks and dreaded what she would find in the crummy hotel vending machine.

As she emerged into the hallway outside the conference room, she spied a familiar figure leaning against the glass and pushing the buttons on the vending machine. Her old journalism school classmate filled out a little since college, mostly in the shoulders, and his hair wasn't quite as sun-streaked as it used to be. He traded in his cargo shorts and band T-shirts for the classic weatherman ensemble of belted, black slacks and a button-down shirt rolled at the sleeves. Other than that, he appeared to be the same Mark Fox who made her feel invisible all those years ago, only more handsome and annoying somehow. The same Mark Fox who was at that very moment helping himself to the last package of trail mix.

Chapter Four

"Taking the last healthy snack for yourself, I see?"

Mark lifted his head, still bleary eyed from being so rudely woken from his nap. He took a moment to register the question. He stared at the mixed package of sunflower seeds, peanuts, raisins and cashews in his hand and then up at a very angry Melody Orlean.

"Looked like the best option." He shrugged. "There's a whole bunch of other stuff in there. Pretzels, chips, cookies …those are vegan, I think."

"Gross." Melody rolled her eyes and turned back toward the conference room door.

Mark followed at her heels, crunching his trail mix. He couldn't guess what he ever did to make this touchy, albeit *gorgeous,* meteorologist so mad, but now, he had just as much cause to be mad at her, too. Her noisy arrival ruined his nap. "I don't think the kitchen is closed yet. I bet Russel can help you get some room service."

"Ha!" She muttered something inaudible under her breath and sauntered toward her cot.

"Oh wait, I think I have some beef jerky. You want some?"

"No thank you," she shouted. "I'm not even hungry."

"You know, we'll be sharing the same space for a while. We can play nice." Mark flopped on his cot. A cold chill seeped into his gut as if all the air was sucked from the room. Even with her back to him, Mark could recognize the body language of a woman who was angry. Melody practically skidded to a full stop, squared her shoulders, straightened her back, and stood tall as she turned with pink cheeks and a sparkle of rage in her eye. If he wasn't already put off by her death stare, he might have almost been turned on by her reaction.

Melody stormed from her corner of the conference room.

Her topaz eyes were aflame as she leaned over him, the rage bouncing off her body in waves. Mark continued to lounge and munch on his trail mix as he tried his best not to look intimidated, which he was. Intimidated and intrigued all at once.

"Let's make *one* thing clear." She pointed her finger and waved it in his direction. "*We* are not here to make nice. *W*e are here to work. And that's *exactly* what *we* intend to do."

Ty and Jade gave each other twin side-eyes and frowns from the far end of the room, as a church-like quiet entered the room.

A prickly heat crawled up his neck toward his face, but Mark couldn't let himself show any kind of emotion whatsoever. Instead of reacting, he shrugged his shoulders and popped an almond in his mouth in the most indifferent way possible. "Well, I will be sure to let you and the royal 'we' get to work then."

"Good." Melody turned heel again, her hair flying around her head.

Mark finally allowed himself to exhale, low and slow like a pressurized valve. Melody Orlean was every bit as scary as she was beautiful, but Mark didn't intend to let her know that. After all, he and Jade *did* get to the resort first, and from the sounds of the storm outside, no one would be leaving anytime soon.

"Ty, let's go try to get a shot out by the beach before this picks up." Melody spoke up loud enough for everyone in the room to hear.

Mark snickered as Ty rolled his eyes behind Melody's back.

The cameraman shook his head and hauled his gear out the door.

He had to give it to the local meteorologist; she certainly could assert herself, if not in an abrasive sort of way. Mark shook his own head at the notion that at least he wasn't the only one being affected by Hurricane Melody.

The small storm crew from WINK News packed up their gear on the other side of the shared conference room, and things grew quiet again. Mark lay back in his rollout cot and resumed his pre-show time relaxation ritual. Now that his nap was so rudely interrupted and his pulse jacked up well over the suggested rate, it would be impossible to fall back asleep.

Instead, Mark decided to rehearse his script for the eleven o'clock segment that night and obsessively cycled through all of the National Weather Service websites he needed to cross-reference with. He wasn't nervous about driving down to cover the hurricane some twelve hours earlier, but the storm took an uncharacteristic sharp right turn since the morning. The eye was now a tight bowling ball coming in for a strike, and Fort Myers Beach was the ten pins.

Even though Mark struggled to rehearse his storm

predictions in his mind, as he lay on his cot for the remainder of his rest period, he couldn't clear his racing thoughts. He tried to come up with fresh new ways to explain "storm surge" and "forward velocity" but all he could think of was Melody and her angry, flashing, golden-brown eyes. The more he thought about the feisty, fashionable meteorologist in the see-through rain slicker, the angrier he got until all he could think about was showing her he wouldn't be moved. It was every meteorologist for themselves when it came to the biggest storm of the decade. Mark Fox was determined to come out on top.

****

Mark stared at his waterproof pancake makeup later that evening in the Mali Kai conference room and frowned at his reflection. He was sick of wearing it, and considering the conditions outside, it seemed useless to get into full makeup anyway. The wind and rain were whipping and pouring outside, accelerating in intensity just as Mark predicted. Hurricane Loraine was slow moving over the Gulf of Mexico, which was a bad thing. The longer the storm brewed and took its time moving over the warm gulf waters, the larger the hurricane got and the stronger the winds became.

Melody and Ty returned from their eight o'clock filming session soaked and windswept to no one's surprise.

Mark didn't even try to make small talk or pretend to be pleasant, and neither did Melody, though he could tell from her expression the storm was more intense than she anticipated too.

The meteorologist and her cameraman only returned to the conference room for a change of dry clothes but hadn't show their faces since.

"I remember her now." Mark frowned in the portable lighted mirror.

Jade looked up from her camera equipment at his reflection. "Who, Melody?"

"Yeah." He sniffed. "We went to the same small journalism school. She was really quiet and reserved back then."

"She's definitely not quiet now." Jade laughed.

"No, she's completely different. The only time she ever talked to me was right before graduation. Actually, that's how I figured out who she was." Mark cast his mind back to that day and was barely able to recall the incident where Melody and he first faced off so long ago. Their small class of 103 graduating students, all dressed in green and gold caps and gowns, lined up along the waterfront in downtown St. Petersburg. He received word from the head producer at Bay News 9 that his summer internship was approved, and he stood around and bragged to his friends about it. He probably downed five or six beers by then and wasn't exactly in the best state when they collided. He couldn't really blame Melody for being mad. He did tear her graduation gown, after all.

Jade's brows rose. "What did she say?"

Mark laughed through his nose and frowned, then shook his head. "She was the girl who told me off in front of my entire graduating class."

"What?" Jade laughed.

"Yup," he said. "I might have been a little drunk. I might also have stepped on her graduation gown and ripped it."

"*No.*" Jade's mouth gaped wide.

"Yeah," he said. "Unfortunately."

"So she's hated you for a long time then?" Jade grinned and secured the camera's rain jacket. "I can't imagine why."

"You think I'm bad now? I don't even want to think about how brainless I was at twenty-one."

"That was an accident, though," Jade said. "Do you think there was something else she was mad at you for?"

"Who knows? I had only one thing on my mind back then, and it wasn't school or my career. I probably did something to deserve it."

"So if you weren't focused on school or your career, how did you get a job at Bay News 9 right out of college?" Jade pulled a poncho over her head.

"My dad's friend helped me get the internship." He shrugged. "Once my foot was in the door, I was good to go. Too bad the job turned into a life sentence."

Jade sighed and shook her head.

Mark chuckled. "White dude problems, am I right?"

"Well, at least you're self-aware." Jade gave him a pat on the shoulder. "Come on. Let's go get this over with. I've got a bottle of tequila in my duffle with our names on it."

"Jade, you are an angel in front of and behind the lens." In his soaked loafers and rain jacket, Mark Fox strode out of the conference room with his bravado reignited, his complexion not so camera-ready, and his mind tuned into the weather. He was so focused that he failed to look where he was going. Instead, Mark barreled around the corner and smacked face-first into the forehead of one Melody Orlean.

Chapter Five

"Ow!" Melody blinked away the stars in her eyes and stumbled backward, the pain in her forehead sharp and blunt all at once. She rubbed at the space just below her hairline and winced, instantly realizing full-well what a direct hit to the face meant. She exhaled and glared up as she rubbed at the sore spot on her head. Melody was annoyed but not surprised to see the equally banged-up cranium of Bay News 9 weather darling, Mark Fox. "Great." She frowned from underneath the palm of her hand. "This should look nice on air."

"Ow." His stupid, chiseled features were contorted in pain. "Are you okay?"

"I'm fine." She huffed. "Excuse me." Melody pushed past Mark, eager to get a good look at the damage his giant head did to her face. She had enjoyed a well-deserved margarita with Ty to wind down after their first official segment was complete and was cheerfully buzzed up until that point. They caught the saintly kitchen manager of the Mali Kai before she left to evacuate, desperate for some kind of sustenance to get through the next twenty-four to forty-eight hours.

Sally hooked Melody and Ty up with an industrial bag of tortilla chips plus an entire cooler of yogurt, fruit, and hard-boiled eggs intended for the resort's daily continental breakfast.

Since all of the guests were gone, the breakfast buffet goodies were all theirs. Now, full of tequila and corn chips, Melody was in much better spirits and feeling more generous about her predicament with the arrogant Mr. Fox. More generous, that is, until they literally butted heads.

"Talk about adding injury to insult," Melody grumbled and plopped on her cot.

Ty wheeled over the cooler of food and assessed the damage. He took Melody's chin in his hand and brushed her hair from her eyes.

The grimace on his face told her everything she needed to know.

"You're gonna want to put some ice on that, babe." He glanced around the room. "Be right back." Ty returned after a moment with a hand towel and filled the cloth with ice from the cooler. He held it out.

Melody pressed the DIY ice pack to her rapidly developing bump. "I'm afraid to look."

"If you ice it, it'll probably be fine in the morning." Ty nodded and gave her a wide-eyed look.

"*Ty,*" she whined. "Why is this my life?"

"Listen." Ty helped himself to an apple from the cooler. "This is just a little blip. You did great out there today."

"No. I mean Mark. This is torture."

"You want another margarita? Sally showed me where the sour mix was."

"I'll be fine." Melody managed a wry smile. "I don't need to be banged up *and* hungover for the 6:00 a.m. show tomorrow."

"Okay." Ty looked over his shoulder. "If you're all right, I'm probably going to hang out with Jade after

27

they are done filming. I'm not ready for bed yet."

"Sounds good." Melody yawned and dug around inside her tote bag. "I'll set my phone for 5:00 a.m. I'm gonna pass out now."

"You sure you're gonna be okay?"

"Positive." Melody gave him a thumbs-up.

Ty waved and disappeared through the conference room doors.

Finally alone, Melody flopped back on her cot in defeat. She needed to be awake again in a little over six hours *and* find a way to sleep, knowing Mark would be on the other side of the room and sharing the same circulated air-conditioning. Maybe a second margarita would have been a good idea, after all.

Melody padded across the hall with her tote bag in hand to the restroom, making sure to avoid the mirror. She already knew how bad the bump looked; she didn't need to torture herself with the evidence right before bed. Melody brushed her teeth, washed her face, and said a silent prayer that her forehead wouldn't look as bad as she imagined for filming the next day. The lights in the bathroom flickered, and another loud boom of thunder sounded overhead, causing her shoulders to tighten. Melody gathered up her things and made a mental note to call her mother in the morning before the power went out for good.

The storm continued to rage outside, and Melody set her earbuds in place and secured her sleep mask. She settled in for the night on her cot in the corner of the Mali Kai conference room and tried not to think about how the biggest storm in recent history was headed their way. Even though the coverage would be an amazing boost for her career, the storm was sure to be bad for everyone in southwest Florida. She tried not to think about how Mark Fox would probably one-up her and make the next day or so a living nightmare with his exposed forearms and easy, cool-guy personality. Melody eventually drifted off that night as Hurricane Lorraine continued to crawl toward Fort Myers Beach with an ever-tightening eye.

****

"How does it look?" Melody emerged from the women's bathroom the following morning at five-thirty tired, aggravated, and sporting a concealed circular blue and green bruise in the dead center of her forehead. As she slathered on a layer of thick, theater-grade foundation, Melody laughed to herself, consoled by the fact Mark Fox's forehead probably looked twice as bad as hers.

"Looks great." The corners of Ty's mouth turned down as one eyebrow rose. "You can barely see anything."

"Liar." Melody returned to the bathroom and glanced in the mirror again. Ty's expression said it all. No amount of makeup would cover the bruise on her forehead before she was due to be on air. "Ty, what am I gonna do?" She ruffled her hair across her forehead in a vain attempt to conceal the bruise. In a brief flash of inspiration, she considered cutting her own bangs to take care of the problem. However, she tried once before when she was twenty-seven after going through an awful breakup and ended up with comically short baby bangs. She knew better than to take shears to her own hair during a crisis.

"You could wear a WINK baseball hat," Ty suggested. "Just pull the bill down low enough and no one would be able to tell."

"*Ugh*." Melody groaned. "I *hate* wearing hats, but that's actually a good idea. Do we still have some in the back of the van?"

"Yeah, it's in that crate of swag. Don't get a white one. It will look awful after two seconds in the rain." Ty tossed the van keys through the air.

Melody caught them with one hand. She headed toward the lobby, still bleary eyed and on edge from her restless night. The first twelve hours at the Mali Kai were difficult and uncomfortable, and between her bruised forehead and the crick in her neck, she was already in a terrible mood. Ty, Jade, and Mark ended up playing cards in the conference room, laughing, drinking, and making so much noise she was driven out to the lobby for some peace.

Melody couldn't sleep anyway; she was too anxious about the storm and too agitated by Mark Fox's very presence to rest. She spent half of the night curled up in an armchair, studying spaghetti models and paying attention to what her favorite indie news reporters said about the storm. Nine out of ten times the independent meteorology websites offered the real scoop on the weather. A dirty secret of the weather trade was that the top meteorologists looked to hobbyist storm chasers for hurricane predictions. Melody respected those independent meteorologists and made sure to cite them as a source whenever they gave her a great tip, unlike some other meteorologists. If anyone knew how hard it was to get recognition and make it to the top, that person was Melody.

The road to becoming a television weather reporter was something of a lifelong dream for Melody. During summer vacations, she would enlist her younger brother to serve as her cameraman and use the family VHS recorder to film mock weather forecasts. Being in front of the camera was something Melody was naturally comfortable with, but even at a young age, she was aware she didn't look like the people on TV. After an awkward start in college, Melody realized an expensive haircut and an even more expensive set of teeth was the price she would have to pay to level up and stand a chance in the meteorology scene.

Melody was aware she was somewhat attractive, even before her minor physical on-air alterations; the way men openly ogled gave her all of the proof she needed in that department. But she wasn't "morning news anchor" attractive in a stereotypical, flawless sort of way, no matter what she wore or how much mascara she layered on. Whenever she would interview and try out for positions in Brunswick, Georgia or Lafayette, Louisiana, she was always passed over for a bubbly blonde whose dress size was in the single digits. She almost lost hope of ever landing a serious meteorology gig until the WINK News job came along.

When Melody covered Hurricane Wilma and Hurricane Charlie, her childhood memories of disastrous Hurricane Andrew came flooding back. Her aunt and her cousins in Homestead lost everything they owned, and one of her uncles even died of exposure to contaminated water afterward. Hurricane Andrew was a tragedy that rocked her family and left her mother shell-shocked to this day. Melody was able to push past her own fears because she always needed to fight for everything she had, and warning people about the dangers of big storms was more important than her pride or giving in to her anxieties.

Melody also found energy in the fact meteorology was by far and large dominated by men who looked like carbon copies of Mark Fox, a ceiling she was dead-set on busting through. Thankfully, in recent years, other tenacious women like herself helped to pave the path for more diversity in meteorology and news media in general. So when the news station in her hometown was looking to add some "fresh faces" to their weather team, curvy Melody Orlean knew she was a shoo-in.

Ty poked his head into the bathroom. "Hey, yo, Mel. You've got to come see the beach."

Melody blinked and made a frowny face at herself in the mirror again. "What is it?"

"The tide is waaaaay out. We gotta hurry. The sun is coming up soon. It's gonna be an amazing shot."

Melody pursed her lips and readied herself for what was sure to be an impressive weather segment. Ty was right. The sunrise that morning probably would be pretty epic and would only be out for a short window of time, and the quiet before the storm was spectacular but often deadly. This break in the weather right before a hurricane hit often fooled people into thinking the storm would miss them or that it wouldn't be so bad.

"Be right out." Melody tucked her WINK News embroidered polo shirt into the waistband of her denim shorts and swiped on one last layer of fuchsia lip color. Bruised forehead or no, Melody was determined to do her best to encourage the people of Fort Myers Beach not to let down their guard as they prepared for Hurricane Lorraine and the horrors the storm was sure to bring.

****

"Folks, I can't stress enough how important it is to evacuate now, especially if you live in a flood zone," Melody spoke in a stern voice, her expression dead serious as she stared into the camera. "If you can't evacuate, please make sure you've stocked up on bottled water, canned goods, and batteries."

Ty motioned a signal that it was time to wrap up as weak rays of light spilled over Melody's shoulder.

Her videographer was right; the morning on the beach was glorious and other-worldly, offering a magical, watercolor sunrise backdrop to a streaky, haphazard, cloud-dappled sky. The beach itself was also breathtaking and unreal, as the tide went out nearly four hundred feet from its usual position overnight. The receded shoreline exposed a bed of fresh, sugary sand brimming with a number of nautical treasures and seashells. While Fort Myers Beach offered an amazing sight that morning, it was also an ominous one. When water went out to sea before a hurricane, the sea always charged back in times three. "For WINK News, I'm meteorologist Melody Orlean. Stay with us for more crucial updates on Hurricane Lorraine as they develop."

"And...wrap." Ty signaled to Melody. "Seriously, Mel, look at all of these seashells!"

"I see." She plucked a sand dollar the size of her palm from the sand. "This beach will be flooded with gawkers now when they should be evacuating."

"Well, we can't save everyone." Ty dug a small whelk shell out of the wet sand. "It's up to us to report the dangers, and it's up to society to practice personal responsibility."

"Speaking of dangers." Melody crossed her arms and shook her head. Mark emerged from the Mali Kai hotel pool deck, stomping down the beach with the confident swagger she could easily recognize, even from afar. He was outfitted in a pair of bright, pink-and-orange floral print swim trunks with a ridiculous grin across his face and a giant board under his arm.

As she watched him approach and the details of his half-dressed form came into focus, Melody's lower lip fell away, and her mouth formed into an *O*. A warm, itchy sensation crawled from her collarbone up her neck as he sauntered through the sand toward her and Ty, looking more like the boy she knew in college than the buttoned-up meteorologist he played on air. She blinked away the image of his bare chest but was thankfully saved by a shock of shadowy black and blue under his mop of messy, wheat-colored hair. His forehead bruise was developing nicely. "What are you doing?"

"Good morning to you, too." He nodded toward Ty. "Hey, man. Nice setting for a beauty shot."

"Seriously, *Mark*." She paused for a moment, surprised at the way his name so effortlessly fell from her lips. "Are you going surfing right *now*?"

"Skimboarding," he said. "It's the perfect time. The water is calm, and no one is out here yet."

"Where did you get a board from, man?" Ty slapped him a high five. "I wanna go."

"Gift shop." Mark hitched his thumb back toward the Mali Kai. "Russel hooked me up."

"Don't you have to be on air soon?" Melody's gaze shifted to the sand. She was having a hard time averting her gaze from his tanned shoulders and torso. A tribal tattoo around his left bicep almost made her roll her eyes, but she couldn't stop looking just the same.

"Not until seven. You should come try it." Mark

caught her staring and threw a devilish grin.

"No thanks." She threw back her shoulders and blinked. "Ty, I'll see you in there. Don't forget we have to be on air at nine." Melody trudged toward the hotel through the wet, sloppy sand, her back muscles tight and rigid. Ty and Mark laughed from behind like two old friends. In a way, she was almost jealous of Ty's easygoing attitude and how he and the Bay News 9 meteorologist hit it off. But Ty didn't have the same kind of history with Mark that she did.

As her blood pressure and breathing leveled out, something buzzed. Melody slipped her half-dead phone out of her back pocket to see the smiling image of her mother and the name Linda Orlean on her caller ID. "Hey, Ma." Melody glanced back at the beach. She shook her head as Mark and Ty whooped and ran down the beach like a couple of kids. A tiny stab wedged its way into her heart as she watched them dive into the water.

"Yeah, I'm doing fine." Melody trudged back into the hotel with her phone in one hand and her heart in another. The words came out hollow and automatic as she reassured her mother, but she held out hope for her mother's sake. Melody read the charts and predictions and knew the worst was on its way. She could only trust that her brother boarded up the windows to their childhood home and stocked up on supplies like she said. "It's gonna be okay, Ma." She sighed. If only she knew that it was true. "Everything is going to be just fine."

Chapter Six

"Thanks, man. That was wicked." Mark slapped Ty another high five as the two men laughed and huffed along the receded shoreline of Fort Myers Beach. The sky overhead grew dark, and the wind picked up again in the small window of time he and the WINK News videographer spent skimboarding along the beach. He had an hour at best to enjoy the unnerving, calm morning caused by the brief break in the storm. As he suspected, locals came out in droves to gawk at the newly expanded shoreline and collect shells previously inaccessible and hidden underneath four feet of water. Unfortunately, it was probably far too late for those people to reach safety. Everyone who still remained in the area by that afternoon was sure to be trapped on the beach by Hurricane Lorraine.

"Any time. We're gonna be cooped up in this box for a couple of days at least. Feels good to stretch my legs." Ty offered a warm grin.

"Thanks for being cool." Mark kicked at the sand. "I don't know what Melody's problem is with me. I'm just glad you don't share her sentiment."

"Hey, whatever is going on between you two is your business." Ty shrugged. "I ain't takin' sides."

"Noted. Wanna do another round of poker tonight? I brought cigars, if that's your thing."

"I think I'm good on the cigar, but I'll play cards

again," Ty said. "We'll need something to keep us occupied in between live shots anyway."

"Cool. Catch ya later then." Mark and Ty slapped one last high five for good measure.

Ty jogged toward the back entrance of the Mali Kai where his camera gear was stashed.

Mark pondered whether or not he had time for one last run with the skimboard before he was due to meet with Jade. Getting his blood pumping and his lungs burning was exactly what he needed after a restless, cocktail-filled night. Mark was supposed to go live on air in about thirty minutes and would normally be obsessing about his hair and makeup in front of a mirror. At this point, he didn't give two flips about what he looked like. He rubbed at the bump on his forehead and winced as the memory of the night before came rushing back.

Mark. You idiot.

As if Melody needed *another* reason to hate him, now they both sported twin forehead bruises on account of his clumsiness. At least Mark could take a break from slicking back his hair and wear it casually if he wanted to cover up the mark on his face. Melody, on the other hand, pulled down the brim of a WINK News baseball cap over her forehead to cover up her own bruises while shooting live segments. He would never tell her, but seeing Melody dressed down and in a baseball cap no less was kinda cute.

In a way, Mark was glad he got a bump on the head; it gave him an excuse to let go of his occupational vanity and look a little shabbier than usual. He was gradually growing weary of the buttoned-up aesthetic the meteorology life required and yearned to return to his authentic self. The real Mark Fox wore comfortable clothes and tucked his unruly hair under a hat whenever possible. The real Mark Fox didn't shave every day or obsessively whiten his teeth or wear makeup. Now, with a major hurricane on the way, Mark decided maybe now was the time to give his fans a taste of what he was really like.

Mark glanced up at the sky and hoped he and Jade would have enough time to get ready for their opening shot. It was a risk, but he wanted to try filming his 7:00 a.m. show in the loud swim trunks he found in the Mali Kai gift shop to mix up things a bit. He would put on a tank top in front of the camera, of course, but Mark suspected the Bay News 9's social media accounts would still get a lot of pings after his early morning show regarding his casual look. Heck, he might even do a little skimboarding at the end of the segment to tick off his producers.

A rumble in the distance sent a thrill of excitement up Mark's spine. The storm the night before was something of a warm-up for the main event; the first wave of tropical weather was meant to serve as a warning for the real storm just beyond the horizon. Mark had covered tropical storms and hurricanes for over a decade now, and each time his body hummed with excitement to witness the extreme power of Mother Nature. Everything about covering hurricanes from feeling the barometric pressure around him drop to smelling the salt of the sea on the wind gave him life. Being in the thick of a storm was better than any rollercoaster ride or adrenaline-fueled activity. Chasing storms gave Mark Fox a natural high.

Mark relaxed a little at the sight of Jade trudging

toward the shoreline with her gear in hand. He already memorized his quick, two-minute script earlier in the morning and only needed to give a brief update with the usual warning about evacuating and stocking up on supplies. He was also planning a plug for his big, seven-minute segment at 9:00 a.m. when he would announce around-the-clock coverage "on the nines" until Hurricane Lorraine passed.

Another low rumble echoed down the beach as Mark pulled a Mali Kai logo tank top over his head. He propped his hands on his hips and stared at the stormy sky overhead, looking forward to his first appearance of the day.

****

After a quick meal of leftover continental breakfast yogurt and fruit, Mark showered and took a moment to relax in the shared conference room. Despite starting the day out right with skimboarding and a bright outlook, he still ended feeling defeated and deflated. His producer, Angela, was *not* pleased by his surfer guy on-air aesthetic, though Mark was half expecting to get his wrist slapped for going off script. The text from her on his work phone proved that would be the case.

—Fox, what's with the surfer-boy aesthetic? Get it together and put on a tie for the next segment. If you're not going to act like a professional, you might want to look for another meteorology job —

A snort escaped from his nose. Mark deleted the text and rolled his eyes. *Good. Maybe I will.* Mark kicked back on his cot and chuckled to himself as he scrolled through the Bay News 9 social media accounts and immediately realized how wrong Angela was about his skimboarding segment. Dozens and dozens of comments came pouring into the news station's social media feeds, from fans of all ages, and all with comments about *him*. His cheeks heated at some of the more racy remarks, including the ones requesting he take off his tank top next time.

Melody made herself scarce after their run-in on the beach, something that didn't surprise Mark in the least. On his way back in from filming that morning, Mark passed the gym by the pool and spied her jogging on the treadmill, her short crop of dark, wavy hair bouncing along in time with her steps. He averted his gaze and forced his legs to move at the sight of her. He was tempted to stand and watch Melody run, especially since she looked so nice from behind. Mark Fox might be a lot of things, but a creeper wasn't one of them.

Around nine a.m., Melody strode back into their shared conference room dressed in a simple, blue wrap dress, her hair and skin still damp from a shower. A fresh and heady mix of eucalyptus and something soft and floral wafted in with her and filled the room. The calming fragrance soothed and intrigued him all at once. Something stirred inside that he couldn't quite put his finger on. Why, oh, why did she have to hate him?

"So, um…how's your face?" Mark cringed at his opening line, though it worked at getting her attention.

"What do you think?" Melody stopped dead in her tracks and turned.

Her glare could strip paint off walls. Melody wore a good amount of heavy-duty makeup, but no amount of foundation or concealer could disguise the very visible lump settled above her brow. Mark bit his lower lip. "I mean…it could be worse, right? One time I sneezed live on air, and, well, let's just say, it wasn't pretty."

"Gross." A hint of a smile crept in at the corner of her mouth. "I heard about that."

"*Everyone* heard about that." Mark rolled his eyes. "It was the snot heard round the world. I think that weather segment even made it onto some blooper reel online."

Melody chuckled and turned her back to him.

"Anyways." Mark scratched his chin and flicked his gaze around the room. "I just wanted to apologize for bumping into you last night."

"It's fine."

Mark cleared his throat and dusted off his hands on his gray dress pants. Things were still clearly *not* fine. "Well, gotta get out there again. Getting ready to announce my hourly *Weather on the Nine's* segment."

"Won't be much to report until later this evening." Melody didn't look at him. "Just regurgitating the same information and building hype."

"That's what we do though, right?"

"Maybe that's what *you* do." She turned to face him. "Our job should be about warning against the dangers of the storm. We should be focused on informing the public so they don't get hurt or end up dead."

"Well, of course we do that, *too*." Mark's chest tightened, and his ears flamed as he digested her words. What kind of meteorologist did she think he was? Sure, he filmed a risky, maybe even unethical segment at the end of his weather report where he was literally skimboarding before a storm. Sure, he wasn't always the most serious meteorologist on air. But getting the facts right was important, and so was the safety of his viewers. Was it really so bad if he also had a little fun in the process? "Well, I'm going out there." He swallowed his words. "Good luck."

"See ya."

Mark pursed his lips and exhaled a long, slow breath as he left the conference room in search of Jade once again. People didn't usually get under his skin. Mark let situations like this roll off his back and didn't allow himself to get all hung up over snooty news anchors or high-strung producers. However, something about Melody got under his skin. Something that made him want to make her like him. At this rate, the possibility of them becoming friendly, let alone civil, was about as likely as Hurricane Lorraine passing them by.

With his noose of a necktie secured, his hair meticulously parted to the side, and his forecast for the next hour memorized, Mark headed out to the pool to meet Jade for their first hourly shot of the day. Melody's harsh words and insinuations continued to run through his mind, stinging his ego as he strode down the empty hallway of the Mali Kai. He pushed her pretty, angry features out of his head as he memorized wind shear forecasts and storm surge predictions, only to return to intrusive mental images of her soft curves and commanding presence.

As Mark emerged toward the pool deck to kick off his official, round-the-clock hurricane coverage that morning, his thoughts were dominated by the pretty meteorologist. He had to find a way for them to work together and get along. Surely he could find a common ground they could share and some way for him to show her he wasn't a bad guy. Unfortunately for Mark, as he made his way out to the pool, he didn't realize his prime filming spot was already taken, and when Melody Orlean held a grudge, it was usually there to stay.

Chapter Seven

"Really?" Melody stepped out onto the gusty pool deck of the Mali Kai, and her blood pressure spiked almost immediately. The morning dawned soft and quiet, but the winds picked up again just as she predicted, and conditions were only expected to get more intense by the hour. Multiple locations on the resort property were perfect for filming during a storm, like on the beach, for example, or on the balcony overlooking the shoreline. While the weather was still relatively mild, the parking lot in front of the Mali Kai resort sign was even more ideal. But of all of the places on the property to film, *of course* Mark Fox picked the very spot on the pool deck that she and Ty set up some thirty minutes before.

"What?" Mark pulled at his necktie. He exchanged a confused look with his videographer.

Jade shrugged at Melody and Ty.

"We're filming here. We go on in five minutes." Melody clenched her fists, stars exploded in front of her eyes.

"Oh, I'm sorry. I didn't know we were calling dibs on filming locations." Mark rolled his eyes.

"No dibs about it. Ty's gear is right over there," Melody shouted, raising her voice a whole octave. "It's *obvious* we were planning to film here."

"How are we supposed to know what time you go

live?" Mark asked.

His ears were beginning to turn a peculiar shade of purple, and almost offset the bruise on this forehead. If Melody wasn't so aggravated, she might have taken a little bit of pleasure in seeing him writhe. "You know, this is exactly why it's not a good idea to share a filming location." Melody pinched the bridge of her nose in between her fingers. "Look, I think we have to set up some boundaries."

"Fine."

"Good." Melody smiled and propped a triumphant hand on her hip. "If you'll excuse us, I need to warm up."

"Well, I never agreed to move from the pool deck." Mark folded his arms across his chest. "We're all ready to go. You're not even set up."

Melody pursed her lips and looked to Ty, who shrugged back with an indifferent expression. Her usually high-spirited, positive videographer was already looking tired and emotionally worn down. A pang of guilt stabbed her right in the gut as she considered her actions over the last few hours. She could sense her feud with Mark was affecting not only herself, but Ty and probably Jade, too. Melody had no problem making Mark Fox suffer, but she didn't want her long-held grudge affecting everyone else during their storm stakeout.

Ty sighed. "Mel, we gotta set up somewhere. Let's just go out on the beach."

"Fine." She huffed and returned her attention to Mark. "We'll pick up this later."

Mark shrugged and stared at the pool, not meeting her gaze.

Melody plodded along behind Ty toward the beach to film another bland storm update. She was tired of the constant mental and verbal sparring between her and Mark. She didn't like it one bit. Melody also knew that standing up for herself was essential, not only in the news media industry, but in life in general. Her integrity was more important than "playing nice" for the sake of not coming across as pushy or problematic. She worked too hard not to make sure she occupied the spaces she deserved and got the things she needed, and no one, especially Mark Fox, would make her doubt that for a moment.

Before they even reached the shoreline, Melody and Ty discovered they were no longer alone on Fort Myers Beach. As she suspected, dozens of locals were out on the beach in the beginning of the storm beachcombing and collecting the array of treasures the receded shoreline exposed. She wanted to scream at all of them to get out of town while they still could. She wanted to make sure each and every one of them were stocked with enough supplies and a safe place to stay because Hurricane Lorraine was no joke. From all of the data she collected, she deduced that this particular storm could potentially be one of the worst in US history. Hurricane Camille topped out at over 190 mile per hour winds in 1969, flattened Mississippi, and killed over two hundred people. Melody sensed the aftermath of this hurricane would prove to be far worse.

"These people don't know what they are in for." Ty shook his head. "The Gulf Coast is not the place to be right now."

"Well it doesn't help when show-offs go out and play in the surf right before a major storm." She huffed,

46

pushing the image of a shirtless Mark from her memory. It wasn't working.

"It's not dangerous out here yet." Ty peered through the viewfinder of his camera. "Besides, it was kinda fun. Good way to blow off steam. You should give it a try."

"I don't have time for fun." She frowned. "Are we ready?"

Ty nodded.

Melody smoothed back her hair against the wind and readied her microphone.

"In five, four, three…" Ty silently mouthed the rest of his countdown. He held up the signal they were ready to go live.

Melody looked back toward the hotel to where Mark was already deep into his own live coverage, no doubt blowing the storm out of proportion and using scare tactics instead of smart weather advice. She wondered how similar their forecasts were, and if he was as worried about the storm as she was.

For the millionth time that morning, Melody pushed Mark Fox from her mind as she focused on the task at hand. "Good morning again. This is Melody Orlean reporting from Fort Myers Beach." She forced a smile into the camera. "We're starting to really see the effects of Hurricane Lorraine now, and as you can see behind me, many people still haven't evacuated."

A dramatic gust of wind blew across the gulf, sending Melody's hair flying back from her face. She blinked as a whirlwind of sand surrounded her, sticking to her lips and licking at her eyes. She shielded her face and maintained a certain level of professionalism as she regurgitated her usual warnings and her newest prediction when the hurricane would make landfall. "So everyone, please, stay vigilant. We're only going to see conditions deteriorate from here on out. Current forecasts show the eye making landfall right here on Fort Myers Beach some time tomorrow evening bringing up to eight feet of storm surge. Conditions will be dangerous to say the least. Until then, stay with WINK News for accurate, up-to-the-minute coverage you can count on." Melody exhaled a sigh of relief.

Ty signaled their live stream ended, and another strong gust of wind blew in.

She shot a scowl of concern at the sky. Hurricane Lorraine had been full of surprises so far, and she wasn't ruling out anything at this point regarding landfall, intensity, speed, or the size of the storm. Melody followed one rule when it came to the weather; expect the unexpected.

A howling blast of sea spray pushed at Melody's and Ty's backs as they wandered up the beach to the safety of the hotel. Melody would have to brave the beach a few more times before the hurricane reared its ugly head, but she still knew the dangers of being exposed during the storm. She also dreaded the uncomfortable but necessary conversation that needed to happen with Mark, an exchange that she realized would probably not end well.

The only solution Melody could think of for making sure they didn't get in each other's way while they were on air was to draw an invisible line right down the center of the hotel. She and Ty would take the north side of the building, and Mark and Jade could film on the south side. This agreement would give him the pool to report from and her access to the main balcony overlooking the beach, which would be better for her needs once the storm picked up anyway. As long as they both stuck to their own respective areas during filming, the rest of their time at the Mali Kai should be smooth sailing.

"I'm gonna go lie down before our next shoot at eleven." Ty yawned. "I only got a few hours of sleep last night."

"Me, too." Melody blinked, her eyelids suddenly heavy. "I have to find Mark first and sort this out. I'm done with all this drama."

"Amen to that. I'll come find you in about an hour."

"Sounds like a plan." Melody couldn't help but feel a little guilty about the way she acted, especially when it came to Ty. He didn't deserve to be roped into the feud with her rival meteorologist, but at this point, it was almost unavoidable. She was stuck between a rock and a hard place; if she stood up for herself, she came off as too aggressive, but if she backed off then she would look weak. Patriarchal hypermasculinity was a common problem Melody ran into in the news world, no matter where she was stationed. She was determined to find a way to make this situation work while they were all stuck together.

Melody searched the main vestibule of the Mali Kai, its empty rattan chairs and cheerful faux tropical plants seeming almost comical. Without the usual bustle of people, she saw the Polynesian-themed resort for what it really was—a sad and lonely box only decorated to look like something special. The wind made itself known once again outside as a sudden gust knocked over a potted palm at the entrance to the hotel.

Melody whipped around her head.

Mark strode across the parking lot toward the Bay News 9 news van, his white button-up billowing in the wind.

"Mark," she yelled. A chest-rattling boom of thunder rumbled overhead.

The Bay News 9 meteorologist turned.

She almost stopped herself from laughing. His makeup was worn off, and a bluish green bruise poked out from his hairline. His expression was flat and stony as she approached, but his shoulders were soft and approachable. She didn't know exactly what she would say or how she could address the very large elephant that sat in between them, but this place was as good as any to start. "I had an idea about how we can make this filming situation work." She shielded her eyes against the wind.

"Oh yeah?" He folded his arms across his chest. "How?"

"I'll take the north side of the building, and you take the south side. You can have the pool. I'll take the grand balcony. We'll call it even."

"Right." He snickered. "The grand balcony is the best spot for filming once the storm really picks up."

"Well, I don't know what else to do!" Melody closed her eyes and sucked in a deep breath. She needed to regain her cool. "What do you suggest? Should we write up a schedule?"

"No. We can just communicate like adults. Talk to each other as the storm progresses. We could work together and help out each other. Did you ever think of that?"

Melody blinked. She didn't consider the possibility

of them working together. She could admit she was very curious about Mark's opinion on wind speeds and what he thought the estimated storm surge could be. She never imagined he would be willing to share that kind of information or collaborate with her.

"Well, I...hadn't really thought about that." Melody stumbled over her words. Another deep rumble overhead caused Melody to jump. She frowned and stared at Mark, his disheveled hair looking off somehow. One-by-one the strands of hair on top of his head stood on end like the worst case of static electricity ever. She was reminded of the glowing plasma ball orbs she and her friends used to play with at the gift shop in the mall; with one touch, the ball would illuminate and look like little snakes of lightning kissing their fingertips. The effect would make their hair stand on end, in exactly the same way Mark's hair reacted now. "Um, Mark." An acrid, panic sensation rose in her throat. "I think we need to get inside."

"Why?" Mark placed a hand on top of his head. His eyes opened wide.

Melody's scalp tingled as her own hair stood straight in long, spiky strands. A whimper slipped from her lips, and her legs lost all feeling as she pieced the clues together a moment too late. The air crackled around them, but they were frozen in fear, their feet planted in the asphalt parking lot under a dark and brooding sky. A brilliant flash of light exploded in the air with a sound that roared, electricity and metal colliding together in an awesome and deafening clap. Lightning touched down like an electric finger piercing through the cloudy morning, landing directly at the base of the Mali Kai resort sign and sending sparks flying through the air.

Melody and Mark screamed in tandem, and his hand shot out to grab her as an electric hand of light touched down in the blink of an eye. A grinding, shrieking noise caught her attention, and she stared up as the vintage Mali Kai sign keeled over with a screech that made Melody's hand fly over her ears.

Mark wound an arm around her chest and pulled her back toward the hotel.

The sign teetered over like a felled redwood tree and landed with a loud, crunching thud on the hood of the Bay News 9 van.

Chapter Eight

"What happened?" Jade emerged from the Mali Kai lobby, her eyes bugging wide. She took in the dramatic storm-damaged parking lot scene laid out before her, and her jaw gaped.

For a moment, no one breathed.

"My van," Jade wailed, and her hands flew to her face.

Mark glanced down at his right forearm, still wrapped around Melody, her mess of fragrant hair tickling his nose and filling his senses. He was acutely aware that even though he cheated death only moments before, all he could think about was her body pressed against his. Mark's heart was still slapping at his chest as each of them gasped to catch their breath, and he released her under the vestibule overhang.

"That came out of nowhere!" Melody's jewel-colored eyes sparkled.

Mark gazed at her, and for a moment, he almost smiled. Florida was the lightning capital of the world, and Mark was no stranger to the awesome power of a lightning strike. However, even he never truly experienced a direct hit; the sensation knocked him for a loop and thrilled him all at the same time. The look of wonder and excitement blended with terror that played out on Melody's face in that moment hit him right in his soft spot. "It almost got us!" Mark turned his attention to Jade. "Are you guys okay?"

"I think so." Melody wobbled on her feet.

"Well, I'm glad for that. But look at our van!"

Jade had a point. The Bay News 9 vehicle was most definitely out of order. The front end was smashed in, and the huge neon hotel sign dating back to the 1960s lay on top of the van. If the Bay News 9 team needed to evacuate now, they were out of luck. Getting a tow truck or a rental car just before or after a hurricane would be close to impossible. "Nothing we can do about that at the moment." He cringed. "You didn't have anything in the van, did you?"

"*No*." Jade pressed her hands to her cheeks. "We're trapped here, aren't we?"

"Ty and I can get you guys out of here if we need to move." Melody stared at the storm wreckage. "If things get bad, we can all go in our van."

Mark did a double take. Was Melody Orlean actually being... nice?

"Well, it probably won't come to that." He cleared his throat. "Thank you, though. For the offer."

"Yeah." She nodded. "I think I need to go lie down for a bit."

Her voice was soft, her eyes hazy as though she were in a trance.

"Okay." Mark ran his hands through his hair. He looked back at the ruined van and hotel sign and his lips spread into a wide grin. "Jade, go get the camera." He rubbed together his hands. "This will be the perfect backdrop to our next live news segment."

****

Mark spent the following hour writing up a quick script on the dangers of lightning before, during, and after a hurricane. His provocative coverage would likely land him national news recognition, maybe even *global* news recognition. He only wished Jade was around to catch it all live on film. Mark reminded himself to get in touch with the head of hotel security to see if they could find any CCTV footage of the lightning strike. He would have to move fast to get the footage of the destruction.

After he and Jade filmed their ten o'clock segment, they returned to the shared conference room to find Melody and Ty both fast asleep in their respective foldout cots. Mark chuckled to himself at the soft continuous whirr of Melody's snore from all the way across the room. If he wanted to continue their feud, he might be inspired to chide her about her sleeping quirk whenever she woke up. However, after their near-death, lightning crash experience, he viewed her in a whole new light. Making her upset or angry on purpose was not on his to-do list.

With his brain buzzing and tired all at once, Mark decided to lie down and stalk the Bay News 9 social media feeds again. However, before his head even hit the pillow, Mark knew that sleep would be next to impossible that night.

Melody snorted and sat up straight in her cot. Her eyes were wild as she sucked in a gasp of air and scanned the room, her gaze landing on Mark.

He glanced across the room, his forehead creased. "Hey, are you okay?"

"Oh my gosh." She held a hand to her chest, panting. "Sorry, I'm fine. I was just having a nightmare."

"What about?" Mark turned his gaze back to his

phone. He pretended to scroll through his contacts, his gaze flicking to a flush-cheeked Melody.

"It was nothing." She smoothed her hair back with her hands. "I have anxiety dreams during hurricane season sometimes."

"That must be awful. Can I get you anything? Bottle of water or something?"

"No." Melody pulled a peculiar expression. "I'll be fine."

A moment of silence passed between them.

Melody grabbed her own phone and began to scroll, still breathing heavily.

Mark wanted to tell her he suffered from crazy anxiety dreams during hurricane coverage too; dreams that felt real and horrifying all at once. In his dreams, he was usually trapped in the throes of a hurricane just like Dorothy, only without the little dog or tornado. He would spin and spin through time, untethered and out of control. Then all of a sudden, he would wake in a panic and drenched in sweat, his pulse *thud-thud-thudding* in his ear. He didn't want to make Melody's situation about himself, though. He was still earning his way back into her good graces after all. "What time do you go on air again?"

A low rumble of thunder sounded overhead.

Mark's gaze flashed to the ceiling.

"Not until noon." She yawned. "Why?"

Mark stretched and rose from his seat. "I figured we could coordinate filming locations. I have to be on at noon, too."

"Right." She rested her chin in her hand. "Got any suggestions?"

He shrugged. "I would suggest filming out front.

Get the smashed news van in the background. The coverage did well on our station." Mark strolled over to Melody's cot and showed her his phone screen. The Bay News 9 Twitter page featuring the photo of his smashed news van racked up almost ten thousand likes.

"Wow. That does seem like a good idea. Only you guys already covered it. It won't seem fresh."

"Right." He nodded. "But we didn't show the CCTV footage of the actual lightning strike. There was no time. You have time to show it, though, if we can get the video from security."

Melody blinked, a ghost of a smile on her lips. "You would do that for me?"

"Sure. We were both there. We both almost got zapped. It's just as much your story as it is mine."

The suggestion of a smile on the pretty meteorologist's lips turned into a full-fledged grin, but only for a moment.

Melody rose and smoothed out her dress. "That's actually a great idea."

"Cool," he said, looking over his shoulder at Jade. His videographer napped in her own quiet corner. For the moment, they were practically alone.

"Let's go talk to my buddy Russel in security." Mark smirked. "I have a feeling he'll hook us up."

****

"I don't know." Russel leaned back in his chair and scratched at the stubble of hair that grew on his chin over the last twelve hours.

The Mali Kai security guard station appeared to be as ancient as the hotel itself with equipment that looked to be seriously in need of updating. Russel snapped his gum as he rocked in his padded rolling chair with his arms folded across his massive chest and his gaze running up and down Melody's figure again. Russel proved to be a cool guy so far, but not someone that Mark would want to ever tangle with. "Please, Russ? It'll only take a minute. We just need to put in our USB drive and copy over some files. Bing, bang, boom. Done."

"But shouldn't I get clearance for that sorta thing?" Russel scratched his head. "Like, I need permission from my boss, I'm sure."

"Your boss will love it!" Melody chimed in. "It's the best kind of free advertising the hotel could possibly want."

Mark glanced over at Melody and gave her an appreciative grin. "Yeah, man. You'll probably get a raise."

Russel looked over from Melody to Mark and then back at Melody again.

She held out her keychain USB drive and gave him a smile. "Please?"

Russel's tough-guy facade faded, and he unfolded his arms. He looked up at Melody and took her USB keychain with a smile. "Well, I suppose it's probably okay."

"Yes!" Mark pumped his fist in the air. He caught a smirk from Russel.

"If I get in trouble for this, I don't wanna take any heat." Russel waved the USB at them.

"No, no. Of course not," Mark said. "Honestly, everyone will be so grateful."

"Mmm. Okay." Russel grumbled and inserted the USB into the hotel's office computer and downloaded the grainy, black-and-white footage of the lightning strike. After a few awkward minutes, the file transfer was complete, and Russel returned the key fob to Melody.

"So maybe you'll finally have a drink with me now, huh?"

Russel eyed Melody in a way that Mark recognized all too well. His stomach lurched at the thought of him and the curvaceous news anchor together.

"Oh, well." Melody's face flushed. "We're here on business, so…"

The sick jealousy that sat in his gut flicked a switch inside. The idea alone of Melody being uncomfortable caused his alpha male senses to kick into overdrive. He swooped in and slapped the stunned security guard on the back. "Thanks, buddy! I'll come have a beer with you later, Russ."

"That's not what I…"

Before Russ could get in another word, Mark and Melody made a hasty exit from the security room.

"My treat, pal," Mark said. "I'll come by later. Thanks again!" He opened the door to the security station and escorted Melody through. He shut out Russel's muffled protests behind him with a triumphant slam of the door.

"Thanks." She exhaled a deep, loud breath as they hurried away from the security station.

"For what?" He picked up the pace, struggling to keep up with Melody. She was shorter than he was, but faster.

"For the footage and the USB. And for throwing cold water on Russel. I don't know if he's creepy or if I'm just overly sensitive."

"Oh, Russ?" Mark looked back at the security

room door. "Yeah, I know a bunch of guys like that. Some of them are okay. Some of them aren't. I don't think you're wrong to be cautious."

"The problem is that you usually can't tell until it's too late." She held up the USB and grinned.

"Yeah, well the same can be said of the women I've dated, too. One minute, they love me. The next minute, I'm a big jerk, and I have no idea what I did wrong."

"Oh, I have a feeling you know what you did wrong." She offered a sideways smile and paused for a moment before they reached the communal conference room.

Ty and Jade were still both asleep but would have to be woken up soon. Mark couldn't help but notice Melody's eyes scanning his arms and chest as he propped himself up against the doorway.

"Thanks again for this." She batted her thick lashes toward the ceiling. "I gotta go shake Ty and tell him we've got footage of the lightning strike to email to the station. He's going to flip."

"So, maybe we can call it a truce?" Mark extended a hand.

Melody glanced at his outstretched palm, her lips pursed together in a funny sort of smile.

This time she accepted his reach without snarkiness or hesitation. As he anticipated, her hand was smooth and cool to the touch, delicate and feminine in a way that his own hands could never be. Their gazes met as they shook, and a shared current of static electricity connected between them. In that moment, Mark knew one thing for certain; he was in *big* trouble.

Melody sucked in a short, sharp breath and

withdrew. She blinked again and flexed her hand before offering him a smile. "Truce." She nodded. "I'll, um…I'll just go get this to Ty."

She turned and walked into the conference room in a blur of heavenly scented hair and soft, cotton-covered curves. Mark wasn't sure what happened, but whatever it was, his head was no longer screwed on straight. Perhaps the stars realigned. Maybe they entered some kind of alternate reality vortex. By all accounts, it appeared he wasn't in the dog house with Melody Orlean anymore, so he must be doing something right. Even though he was still in the danger zone with Hurricane Lorraine, if Mark wasn't careful, Hurricane Melody was sure to do some serious damage to his heart.

Chapter Nine

Melody sat on the edge of her cot, staring at her text messages and smiling.

Her brother, Austin, stared back from the screen, smiling in a thumbs-up selfie with the boarded-up windows to their childhood home in the background.

She exhaled a sigh of relief, knowing her little brother and mother would be safe riding out the storm in their San Carlos Park neighborhood just a few miles down the road from Fort Myers Beach. Part of her wished she could be home with them to reassure her shell-shocked mother and help her brother, but another part of her was almost glad to be riding out the storm at the Mali Kai.

Melody hated to admit it, but Mark Fox was turning out to be an okay guy, after all. Sure, she caught flashes of the cocky, arrogant, carefree college student she knew all those years ago. But even she recognized that, like her, Mark matured over the years and probably wasn't the same person anymore. Still, she couldn't let go of the past. His actions made life hard for her in a way he couldn't understand. Maybe now, after all this time, she would have the opportunity to get it all off her chest. Mark was trying in his own way to be nice, she supposed. She at least owed him an explanation for why she hated his guts all those years ago.

Another loud rumble sounded overhead, snapping Melody from her hazy memories. Her recent updates from the storm prediction websites and independent meteorologists she followed indicated Hurricane Lorraine would continue on her deadly march, fierce and slow as ever. As of mid-day, the storm made landfall over Cuba as a Category 3 hurricane, leaving a wake of destruction and devastation in its path. Over the next six hours, the storm would sit out in the Gulf, building strength over the warm waters as it made its inevitable descent upon Fort Myers Beach. Melody knew in her heart the storm would elevate to a Category 5 hurricane by the time it made landfall, bringing with it dangerous, destructive wind speeds of 160 miles per hour or more.

Melody and Ty's 3:00 p.m. update drew near, which meant time to scout out a new and interesting filming location. Conditions outside would be dramatically different than their first segment that morning, and her usual balcony setup might no longer suffice. She secured a cup anemometer—a tool meteorologists used to test wind speed—to the resort grand balcony and tracked the data obsessively all afternoon. Within a few short hours, the beach began to experience tropical storm force winds, with some gusts up to sixty miles per hour. In that kind of weather, any projectiles flying through the air became weapons.

"You just about ready?" Ty rubbed his eyes.

Marathon hurricane stakeouts were not for the faint of heart, and when it came to around the clock video coverage, Ty was one of the best. Still, lack of sleep was getting to them all, and her heart went out to her hardworking friend and associate. Melody considered putting on another cup of the instant coffee Sally so graciously provided them. "Yep. Getting my latest forecast together, and then I'll be ready to go." She scanned the model ensembles one last time. Conditions outside were still fair for the moment.

Ty hitched a thumb toward the window. "Still want to shoot out on the balcony?"

Melody nodded. "The wind and rain are picking up again soon. We'll be safest there, but not for much longer. Probably our last time using that spot."

"The station loved that CCTV footage, by the way." Ty shot her appreciative finger guns. "Have you seen the numbers yet?"

"No." Melody pursed her lips together. As a rule, she did not engage in the social media accounts for the various news channels she worked for over the years. She stayed away from the message boards as comments about her appearance were all too common. In that regard, Melody was fine with subscribing to the ignorance-is-bliss model. While plenty of viewers said kind things about her, hateful, negative words from the occasional troll still stung.

"Well, it's on its way to going viral." Ty pulled up WINK's video streaming channel. "Our news segment featuring the van getting hit with the lightning bolt brought in nearly a million views. Anthony said he even got a message about it from NewsBuzz. They're reporting about us on their website and socials."

Melody gritted her teeth. "That's…great."

"So, what's the problem?"

Melody exhaled deeply through her nose. "I don't know. You know how you *think* you want something, but you don't know if you're ready?"

"Like what?"

"Like, I know as a meteorologist I'm putting myself out there. People see me and judge me for what I look like and how I speak. I thought I was tough enough to deal with everything that comes with it on a national level, but I don't know."

"I dig it." Ty shrugged. "That's why I like being *behind* the camera."

"Smart man." She hauled herself off the cot with a groan. "How's my forehead look?"

"Better, actually." He nodded.

"Well, let's get this thing over with. After our six o'clock, Anthony will probably have us doing more hourly updates."

"Yup." Ty checked his camera. "Ready if you are."

Melody glanced at her reflection in her compact mirror one last time and pulled her WINK News baseball cap down over her forehead. She agreed to share the grand balcony with Mark but wasn't sure where he would be filming for his six o'clock forecast and wanted to make sure she was ready. As she and Ty wandered out into the empty hotel lobby, the wind howled just beyond the walls, and adrenaline flooded her veins. Hurricane Lorraine had officially begun to show her powerful, terrible face.

****

"It's really picking up out here now, folks." Melody's hair whipped about her head, finding its way into her eyes and mouth. She made a mental note to find some hair ties ASAP. "If you haven't already, now is the time to take shelter. Bring in your pets and be sure to secure any loose items around your home. Even in tropical storm force winds like we're experiencing

65

now out here on Fort Myers Beach, a kayak oar or a forgotten fishing pole can turn into a dangerous projectile. Please use caution and keep checking in with WINK News for up-to-the-minute coverage you can count on."

Ty gave the thumbs-up signal for the end of their live segment.

Melody removed her baseball cap, and her hair flew in the wind. She *really* wished she had a hair tie at that moment. She smoothed her unruly tresses back under the hat, and as she braced against the high winds, a light smattering of rain stung her cheeks. She turned to look at the Gulf of Mexico, now a gray blob of choppy froth under the overcast sky. Melody blinked and frowned as she looked out on the shore in disbelief. "Is that…Mark?"

Ty set down his camera and leaned against the balcony rail.

Another gust of wind pushed her back and almost knocked off her hat. Sure enough, Mark Fox, in his loud pink-and-orange swim trunks, ran toward the shoreline of the beach with a skimboard in his hands. She stewed inside and could only glare at the scene that unfolded before her eyes.

Mark threw the board into the surf and jumped on, pushing the board into the treacherous water, his body moving and undulating with the waves.

"Why does he insist on being so dangerous?" Melody huffed and turned on her heels. Her heart fluttered in her chest like a little hummingbird, bringing on a new emotion in regards to Mark Fox she didn't expect. Was it anger? Worry? Either way, Melody found herself stomping down the stairs toward the Mali

Kai lobby, determined to go out onto the beach and give him a piece of her mind.

"Where are you going?" Ty's voice boomed through the open, empty staircase.

"I need to stop him," Melody shouted back. She broke into a jog as she slipped through the hotel lobby and out the back door onto the pool deck. The beach was every bit as blustery on the ground as up on the grand balcony, only with more sand whipping at her face and bare legs. A forgotten beach umbrella tumbled across her path, barely missing her as she jumped out of the way. She hugged herself as the rainbow-hued projectile was carried off by the wind and continued down the shoreline, cementing her cause for concern.

Just ahead, laughing and whooping was Mark, his bronzed body twisting and turning to meet the tide.

Mark still managed to retain his boyish good looks after all these years. He certainly filled out in all the right ways, and at this point, Melody found it more and more difficult not to notice. "Mark!" Melody cupped her hands around her mouth and called his name into the wind, the gales whistling and at times howling in her ears. She wasn't even sure if he would hear her, but she enjoyed the sensation of yelling his name just the same. "Mark!"

He turned his head and looked back with his board in his hands and his feet planted in the stormy sea. He smiled and waved, his glaring white teeth standing out against his tanned complexion in the gray afternoon.

A gust of wind ripped through the beach and sent Melody's skirt flying. As she grasped the billowing hemline of her skirt, she spotted Mark's skimboard caught in the wind.

In the blink of an eye, the board smacked him in the face and knocked him to the ground.

"Mark!" Melody fell into a sprint as she ran toward the shoreline, her pulse already jacked up to a dangerous level. By the time she reached him, she saw Mark rubbing at his nose and hauling himself from the ground. "Are you okay?"

"Fine." Mark shook his head and groaned. "Couldn't be better."

"You'll get yourself killed out here!" She planted her fists at her sides. The wind was trying its very hardest to blow her dress clean off her body.

"The storm's not even a Cat 4 yet." He shrugged. "It's totally fine."

"It's *not* totally fine! You know just as well as I do that the riptide is super dangerous right now."

"I'm only skimming along the shoreline. I need to do something. I hate being cooped up on these hurricane stakeouts. Don't you?"

Mark had her there. She did hate the cabin fever side-effects of hunkering down for a storm. But she also recognized they needed to take shelter, even during the beginning stages of a hurricane. "*Fine*, if you want to be irresponsible, then that's on you. But please stay out of my live shots from now on. Playing in the storm is *not* the message I want to send to my viewers." With her skirt clenched in her fists, Melody turned and marched back with her face on fire. She was angry with Mark—*furious*, even—but in a different sort of way now. He was being reckless and stupid and risking his safety, all for the sake of a little bit of fun. For whatever reason, his stupid, thoughtless actions were making her anxiety peak.

"Wait up!"

Melody turned to see Mark running toward the shoreline with a skimboard under his arm.

"Listen, I'm trying real hard here." The wind carried away his voice. "I'm trying to be nice. I'm staying out of your way. It's like I can't do anything right."

"You just think hurricanes are a big joke, don't you?" She stomped through the sand, eager to get away from the worsening conditions. "Just a way to hype up ratings and get people all stirred up and excited."

"You've got me all wrong." He shook his head, his voice rose. "I care. *You're* wound too tight to enjoy *anything*."

Melody whipped around to face him, her lips pursed together and throbbing. Her entire body was hot, and she didn't know if she wanted to give him a good hard smack or do something else all together. Her fingers ached from clutching the hemline of her dress against the wind. If it weren't for the tropical breeze exposing her, who knows where her hands would have landed? "You try to enjoy experiencing this nightmare after living through Hurricane Andrew." She bit her lower lip, determined not to break. "Some people lose everything after a storm. Their homes. Their belongings. Their *lives*."

Mark looked back, his expression screwed up and pinched.

For a split second, Melody almost felt a little pity. *Almost.* How could she ever get someone like Mark Fox, someone who was handed everything on a platter, to understand her life?

"Melody." His voice was softer this time. "I…"

"Forget it." Melody turned toward the hotel, marched past the pool, and back into the hotel lobby, leaving Mark behind. Charcoal-gray clouds continued to sweep across the sky, signaling the end of their break in the weather.

To think someone like Mark Fox would change was ridiculous. To spend any more energy and time worrying about him was a waste. Let him be pulled out to sea and get caught in the undertow. Let an errant piece of driftwood impale him as it flew through the air. What did she care? Mark Fox was an arrogant young man in college, and now he was an arrogant, approaching-middle-age meteorologist. Maybe some things never change.

Melody looked back again to see Mark, standing in the wind, his hair whirling about his head. That same old stab in her heart she always felt toward him, the confused blend of hatred and longing, sank all the way to her stomach. As she stomped back into the hotel, windswept and emotionally drained, Melody wished she could just feel indifferent toward him. Numbness would be light years better than whatever emotion had curled up inside her. On the matter of Mark Fox, Melody wished she could feel nothing at all.

Chapter Ten

Mark's stomach made an embarrassing, audible complaint—a rumbling, gurgling sound so loud it caught Jade's attention.

Jade looked up from her book as they relaxed during their downtime that evening between the six and eleven o'clock news.

They both packed their own respective lunches to tide them over for the weekend, with his cooler full of diet sodas and premade subs and hers with various salads, vegan wraps, and something she called a smoothie bowl. Jade was smart enough to have the forethought to ration her food and was still in good shape meal-wise. Mark was down to one last sandwich.

Apparently, he didn't account for how hungry he would be after being active all day. While skimboarding was all fun and games, the extra work made him want to eat twice as much. Having a big after-workout appetite was a fact which he didn't regret. However, Mark did regret the way he left things with Melody. After some self-reflection, he realized her out-of-line reaction to his skimboard in the storm came from a place of concern. While her delivery was in pure abrasive Melody Orlean fashion, after a while, Mark could sense she wasn't harshing his vibe. The truth was, she didn't want him to get hurt.

He eyed the roast beef and swiss hoagie, knowing

full well if he ate his last sandwich now, he would only have random vending machine snacks to munch on for the duration of the storm. This hurricane wasn't his first rodeo, and he usually planned well in advance and didn't have to worry about something so simple as running out of food. However, Hurricane Lorraine threw everyone in the meteorology industry for a loop. The storm was initially supposed to make landfall in Cuba and then sail back out to the Atlantic Ocean. Instead, it hung a wide left and headed their way, leaving zero time for him or anyone else to plan. Now with the wind and rain in full effect outside, Mark was forced to think on his feet if he wanted to eat. "I'm going to wander into the kitchen and see if Sally left us anything else." Mark clapped together his hands. "I was thinking, maybe I could cook dinner for everyone."

"That would be pretty dope," Jade said. "Just see if there's a meatless option for me and Ty, if you can."

"Noted. Be right back." Mark wandered down the empty hallway of the Mali Kai Hotel and paused for a moment to look out the large back windows leading to the pool. The rain was coming down sideways now, with wind lashing at the fronds on the palm trees that surrounded the exterior. They were in for a long night, and Mark was determined not to make it an awkward one. A community dinner of some kind would surely show Melody he wanted to make amends and might help to cut the tension between them.

As he passed the gym, he couldn't help but notice Melody pounding the treadmill again. This time, he observed her walking with her headphones in and her gaze trained on the stormy beach outside. The reflection of her face in the mirror showed an expression Mark was still struggling to comprehend. Was it anger? Fear? Both? Mark was once again staring and forced his legs to move only a moment too late.

Melody met his gaze in the reflection.

His heart leapt into his throat as her head whipped around.

She turned and hopped off the treadmill with both hands on her hips. "Can I help you?"

"Oh." Mark cleared his throat. "Um…sorry. I didn't want to bother you."

"Well, you did."

"I'm heading to the kitchen to see what Sally left out." He scratched the bridge of his nose. "I thought I could whip up dinner for both of our crews, if you're interested."

Melody blinked and crossed her arms in front of her body. She was dressed in a pair of jogging shoes, bright multi-colored fitness capris, and a matching half-shirt and sports bra. Her crop of dark, wavy hair was piled on top of her head, exposing her strong shoulders and a long, graceful neck.

Mark kept his gaze trained on the Polynesian print carpet out of fear that his expression would give him away.

She cleared her throat. "What kind of dinner?"

"Oh, whatever is in there, I guess." Mark scratched the bridge of his nose. "I didn't plan very well for this storm, and I'm starving. Probably something vegan for Ty and Jade."

Melody nodded. Her scowl softened into an almost-smile. "What time?"

Mark glanced at his wrist watch. "In about an hour? I'll bring it all to the conference room."

"Sounds nice." She inserted her earbuds, then returned to the treadmill. "Thanks."

Mark released a long slow breath and turned away from the open gym door. Something about Melody scared and thrilled him all at once—something that made him want to run the other way or take her in his arms or both. The situation was all very confusing, as though it took three steps forward and two steps back to get anywhere. Mark meandered into the darkened hotel kitchen, crossed his fingers, and said a silent prayer Sally left out something easy to make.

As Russel had promised, a crate of dried goods was there filled with industrial-sized cans of black beans, corn, rice, tuna, and pasta sauce. A package of rice, a box of spaghetti, a small jar of canned mushrooms, and a large container of chicken noodle soup were the only things left on the shelf. Mark frowned at the basic pantry ingredients sufficient enough for survival purposes. Dried rice and noodles were hardly impressive offerings for a peacemaking dinner designed to impress. He scanned the long, stainless-steel countertops in search of something—anything to spice up the meal—and sent a quick mental apology to Sally for what he was about to do.

The pantry at the far wall was stocked with olive oil, onions, garlic, and a full spice rack with dried oregano, basil, and marjoram. Mark collected the items and wrote a note of apology to Sally, promising to replace all the items he used. After rummaging through the drawers and cabinets, Mark got into a groove. He put a stockpot of water on boil and added the spaghetti noodles, then got to work chopping onions and garlic. With the cast iron skillet he found, Mark then sautéed the aromatics in olive oil, adding basil, oregano, and marjoram after they turned from translucent to light golden brown. He then drained and added the canned mushrooms and canned spaghetti sauce but didn't think it was quite right yet. He spied a liter bottle of red wine simply labeled *Red Wine*, shrugged and added a generous splash to the sauce. When the noodles were done cooking and the sauce simmered to his desired level of doneness, Mark wheeled over a rolling cart and placed the still-hot pots on top.

Mark wheeled the fragrant food out of the kitchen and was so proud of his work and distracted that he almost forgot bowls and utensils. He glanced around the kitchen until he spotted forks, plates and in one last burst of inspiration, grabbed four wine glasses, napkins, and the remainder of the wine. He looked back at the culinary mess he made and shook his head. The kitchen was a mess, but hopefully his efforts would be worth it.

As he wheeled his haphazard hurricane dinner down the hallway, Mark crossed his fingers he didn't accidentally add a wrong ingredient to the dinner. He'd never cooked vegan food before, and it hurt him to leave out ground beef or sausage in the sauce for his own personal taste. However, Mark felt it was important to make a meal everyone could enjoy, and this was the best option.

When he entered the conference room, Jade, Ty, and Melody were hard at work tracking the storm and watching various news coverages from around the state.

Action News's Jennifer Green smiled from under a poncho, her long blonde tresses whipping about in the wind with the Sanibel Causeway behind her in a flurry of rain and wind.

Mark cringed. Her disappointed gaze and acid-tongued voice brought on a wave of bad memories. He tried to push away his thoughts as his fellow conference room dwellers tore their gaze from their laptops and screens. "Well, I couldn't find any garlic bread." Mark displayed the extra-large bottle. "But there's wine."

"Oh, thank goodness." Jade slapped closed her laptop screen.

"That smells great." Ty rose from his chair. "Italian?"

"Spaghetti." Mark lifted off the lid of his saucepan, making a fragrant blend of basil, garlic, and tomato fill the air. "And it's all vegan. I used olive oil instead of butter and everything."

"That's really thoughtful, man." Ty patted him on the back. "Thanks."

"We shouldn't be drinking, though." Melody glanced at the dinner and offered an appreciative smile. "But it does smell good."

"A glass of wine with dinner won't be so bad," Ty reasoned.

A loud boom of thunder sounded outside.

"We won't snitch." Mark grinned. "But seriously, please don't feel pressured to drink."

Another even louder clap of thunder shook the walls of the hotel, causing everyone to jump. Something smacked at the back windows overlooking the pool, the uneasy sound traveling down the empty hallway, echoing all the way to the conference room. A second later, another loud crash rattled the entire hotel.

Jade screamed. The walls shook and the overhead lights in the resort extinguished, plunging them into darkness.

Chapter Eleven

"Ouch, my foot!" Melody fumbled for her phone in the dark, desperate to find the flashlight app and illuminate their current situation. She fully anticipated the hotel might lose power at some point, but not in the conference room. Her producer chose the Mali Kai because he was certain the hotel would be equipped with backup generators to help them keep their laptops and gear going wherever they set up camp for the storm. Apparently, that part of the deal was not true.

Mark's face glowed in the dark, his eyes wild as he tapped at his screen. He held his phone to his face as it rang in the dark.

Ty and Jade shuffled and fumbled for their own electronic devices.

Melody craned her neck to listen. A small, gruff voice said "hullo" on the other end of Mark's phone.

"Hey, Russ!" Mark affected his on-air charm. "Yeah, all dark over here, too. I was wondering when we could get those generators going?"

Melody bit her lower lip and grabbed the emergency plastic tote Ty brought in from their van. In it was a first aid kit, thermal blankets, flashlights, a length of rope, and a multi-tool device. However, the tealight candles and matches she was looking for were stashed at the bottom. She rummaged through the tote and brought them over to one of the round tables left set up in the conference room and lit three of the tealights.

Jade and Ty scrambled to check their gear and make sure everything was juiced with enough power for the next live taping.

Mark talked to the security guard and considered the best way to make the most of their current situation.

Amid all of the chaos, Melody laid out the plates, wine glasses, and silverware and set the spaghetti, sauce, and bottle of wine in the middle of the table. She stood back and propped her hands on her hips, satisfied with her impromptu dinner set up.

"Well, if that's the best you can do. Thanks, Russ." Mark returned his phone to his pocket and exhaled.

Jade frowned. "So, what's the verdict?"

"He says it might be an hour or more until he can get the generators going." Mark slumped into a chair at the table. "Hey, this looks nice."

Ty and Jade put away their gear and joined Mark and Melody at the table.

When everyone was seated, Melody dished out heaping servings of the still-hot spaghetti. "You know what?" Melody spooned a serving of spaghetti sauce on Mark's plate. "I think I'm gonna need that glass of wine, after all."

****

"And then, Jennifer Green *threw* the microphone at his head!" Jade and Melody shared a snort laugh.

Mark peeked back over the rim of his wine glass and made a face.

The two women continued to cackle as Melody pictured the furious, petite meteorologist slinging insults and reporting gear at Mark. "What made her so angry?" Melody examined her empty wine glass in the

78

candlelight.

Mark frowned and folded his hands in front of him. "I didn't know her full name."

A burst of laughter filled the air as Mark hung his head.

"How long did you two date?" Jade let out one last laugh and wiped a tear from her eye.

"Only a month!" Mark refilled his glass. "How was I supposed to know her middle name? She never told me."

Melody extended her glass toward him. "Well, I bet you never asked, either."

"True." He nodded and poured a generous refill. "To be fair, maybe I just didn't care. I don't think I deserved getting microphone-whipped though."

Melody took a deep sip from her refreshed cup. "Agreed. There's no reason to ever resort to violence. I'm sorry I laughed."

"Yeah, yeah." Mark pushed away his empty plate. He wished he hadn't eaten so fast.

"That was a pretty good dinner." Ty lifted his glass. "To new friends, vegan dinners, and Hurricane Lorraine."

"I'll drink to that." Jade lifted her glass.

"Well, some of us aren't exactly *new* friends." Mark glanced at Melody, his arms folded across his chest.

"That's right," Ty said. "Jade and I knew each other in school."

"Melody and I knew each other, too." Mark tilted his head to one side.

"A fact which I think we should forget." Melody raised her glass and clinked hers together with Jade's.

She was not anxious to ruin the cozy mood of their candlelight dinner by bringing up the past.

"Aw, c'mon." Ty crossed his arms at his chest. "We should get to know each other. What's the history between you two?"

"Mmm mmm." Melody shook her head. "Nope. Pass."

"Fine, I'll go." Ty rolled his eyes. "Hi, my name is Tyson Pierce from Park City. That's Park City, Kansas, not Park City, Utah. It's a little town just outside of Wichita. Oh, what else… I graduated from Full Sail because I thought I would grow up to direct these beautiful indie films. Instead, I fell in love with a boy from Fort Myers and decided to take a job here at WINK." Ty gulped his wine and signaled for a refill.

Melody stretched across the table with the giant bottle of wine and gladly obliged.

"I'll go next." Jade dabbed her lips with a napkin. "Hi, I'm Jade. I went to Full Sail with Ty. I, too, thought I was going to get into indie filmmaking but landed in television news instead. I live in Tampa with my dog, Oliver. I play disc golf on my days off, and I'm trying to learn Spanish. Oh, also, I am very happy and content to be blissfully and eternally single."

"Good for you." Melody raised her glass in appreciation. She turned her attention to Mark, as a smirk settled on her lips. "What about you, Fox?"

"Me?" Mark cleared his throat. "What *about* me?"

"What's your story?" Melody propped her elbows on the table and rested her chin on the palms of her hands. The wine and candlelight were dulling her sharp edges, making her even bolder than usual. The alcohol was also blurring the line between professionalism and her waning dislike for Mark Fox.

"Oh well, Melody—as you know—I graduated from USF with a Journalism degree and then immediately got to work at Bay News 9, where I've been ever since. I don't have too many other hobbies besides storm chasing and my guitar sometimes. You all know about Jennifer Green, but that was over a year ago. I'm not seeing anyone right now."

As the sounds of the storm raged outside, the group of new friends grew silent.

Ty and Melody exchanged worried glances. A boom of thunder shook through the quiet of their dinner.

Ty turned to Melody. "What about you, Mel?"

Melody pursed her mouth and blew a deep breath from her lips in a sort of dejected raspberry. She twirled the last of her spaghetti noodles on her fork and shrugged. "I got divorced last fall."

Another loud crash of thunder broke through the silent little dinner group.

Melody sucked a deep breath. Perhaps she was being a little too open and honest with her new friends. "Sorry, I know it's a bummer, but it's true. It's kind of been a bad year for me."

"That's okay." Jade reached across the table and offered Melody a side-hug.

Melody managed a sad sort of smile. "After we separated, my mom got sick. She and my brother live just down the road. Anyway, my family needed some help, so I decided to apply for the job at WINK, and now, here I am."

"Aw, babe." Ty pulled her into a hug. "I had no idea."

Melody accepted her friend's embrace, her senses still dulled by the wine. She pulled away from Ty and shrugged, unable to look Mark in the eye. She hoped he wouldn't come over and hug her next. She might not be able to contain herself if he did. "I haven't really talked to anyone at the station about all that yet." She wiped at the corner of her eye. "Great, now I need to redo my mascara."

"I'm sorry to hear all that." Mark played with his napkin and glanced at Melody under heavy brows.

"That's life, right?" Melody let out a dark chuckle. "One minute you're on your way to an interview with The Weather Channel, the next minute your mom is having a stroke. What do you do?"

"You had an interview with The Weather Channel?" Mark met her gaze. His face was screwed in an uncharacteristic sort of way.

"Yeah?" She shrugged. "Is that so shocking?"

"No. Of course not. I'm wildly jealous, that's all."

"Well, don't be." She sighed. "I don't know that I'm cut out for all this anyway."

"What do you mean?" Mark leaned forward. "You're a great meteorologist."

Melody snorted. He was probably paying her lip service, but her cheeks flushed at the compliment all the same. "It's just that…"

As Melody was about to speak, the conference room lights flickered back to life. A low, eclectic hum whirred power through the hotel again, signaling the end of their candlelit dinner.

"Oh, thank goodness." Jade stood and stretched.

"Russ is the man." Mark collected the plates. "I guess I better go clean up the kitchen before our six o'clock show."

Melody looked at the time on her phone; it was already a quarter past five. She stood and rocked back on her heels a bit, as the two, or was it three?, glasses of red wine she consumed with their spaghetti dinner took full effect. "I'll help. Ty, I'll meet you back at the grand balcony at 5:55?"

"Sounds good," Ty said. "Don't forget to bring your poncho."

"Noted." Melody wobbled a bit as she loaded the empty wine bottle, roll of paper towels, and spaghetti bowl onto the cart.

"I've got this." Mark wedged himself in between her and the dinner cart.

Her stomach flipped as his hip bumped against hers. For a moment, her heart swelled at the idea of working with him side by side. Must have been the wine. "But you made dinner." A sly smile crept into the corner of her mouth. "You shouldn't have to do all the cleaning up, too."

"Trust me." He stared at the floor and shook his head. "It's an embarrassing mess in there. I wouldn't want you to have to deal with it."

"Oh." Melody deflated. "Well, if you insist. Where are you filming your next segment?"

"Pool patio. Right, Jade?"

"Yup." Jade flashed a thumbs-up from behind her laptop screen.

Melody dusted her hands and glanced around the room. "I guess I'll just go obsess over the latest storm models then. Thanks for dinner again."

"My pleasure," Mark said. "I can make beans and rice for dinner tomorrow night, as long as the generators hold up."

"That would be nice. I'll let you know if I spot any major changes on the Doppler."

"Thanks." A strange sort of smile played out across Mark's lips as he disappeared from the conference room.

A pang of disappointment settled into her chest as he wheeled their pile of dirty dishes. Maybe it was the wine really was working on her, but she found herself wishing she was following Mark to the kitchen to help wash dishes of all things. She shook the idea from her head, realizing she most definitely needed to brew a cup of coffee, not only to wake up for her next live taping, but also to clear any notions of Mark Fox from her brain.

Even though one spaghetti dinner wouldn't make up for a lifetime of disappointment, Melody admitted to herself their communal dinner was pretty nice. Mark was doing his best to make amends, in the signature, charming way she used to be able to see right through. Still, her long-held grudge against him wasn't easy to reconcile.

As she prepared for her forecast that evening, Melody trolled the Bay News 9 social media feeds searching for mentions about Mark. She smiled at the hundreds of fans who left heart-filled emojis and suggestive comments at his skimboarding in the storm video. She viewed the video once, twice, and then a third time before throwing her cell phone on her cot in a state of semi-panic.

A cold chill flooded Melody's veins, down through her fingertips, and all the way to her toes as something inside her clicked. Her jaw clenched, her pulse elevated ever so slightly, and her breath came in low, shallow puffs of air as she closed her eyes and pushed out the lurid, intrusive thoughts that wouldn't be ignored. The realization of what was going on inside her head and heart would be contained and forgotten by time no more.

Oh my gosh. She gasped, and her eyes flew open wide. *I think I like Mark Fox.*

Chapter Twelve

Hurricane Lorraine proved to be full of surprises, not only in terms of the actual hurricane that was happening right outside the walls of the Mali Kai, but in the storm going on inside Mark's head and heart. Melody Orlean came in fast and hard, forcing him to face the parts of himself he didn't like and test his professionalism to the utmost limits. Normally, Mark would distance and distract himself, but with work to be done and the weather raging outside, he had nowhere to run and hide, not only from Melody, but from himself.

Near midnight, the crew enjoyed a break in between their eleven o'clock live coverage. Both meteorology teams were due for a 6:00 a.m. update and should have been using their downtime to rest, but Mark couldn't sleep as the hurricane approached, even if he tried. He always felt like a kid again during the hours before a storm making landfall; the same feeling of anticipation he remembered experiencing on Christmas Eve or whenever he knew a big vacation was coming up. Watching a hurricane develop thrilled him and helped him regain the sense of wonder he lost long ago. In a world where everything was stable and predictable, the weather was still wild and full of surprises and was maybe one of the reasons Mark loved meteorology so much.

The hurricane stalled in the Gulf of Mexico,

picking up wind speed but not moving ashore as it hovered over the warm body of water. The outermost bands of the storm were now scheduled to reach Fort Myers Beach in the early morning hours, bringing winds in excess of seventy miles per hour. Both crews buzzed with excitement, unable to sleep, too busy volleying between staring out the window at the power of the storm and tracking new forecasts as they came in.

Ty and Jade took turns brewing coffee as everyone worked together in one big group, pooling resources.

Mark already knew Melody was a great meteorologist with a commanding on-air presence, but watching her work behind the scenes was even more intimidating. He couldn't contain a smile as she turned to him with her latest findings.

"You see that new storm surge forecast?" She pointed to the screen.

"Ten feet! The original forecast only predicted four feet." Mark ran his hands through his hair. "That's unreal. Hurricane Charley brought in like eight feet of storm surge."

"I know." Melody tapped at the keyboard on her laptop. "The beach here is around three feet above sea level, and the Mali Kai is elevated another three feet. We're going to be waist-deep in water."

"We have to tell Russel." Mark glanced wildly around the conference room. "Maybe he can get us rooms on the second floor?"

"That's what I was thinking." Melody nodded. "Just in case. Hopefully, the storm surge predictions are wrong, but I don't want to chance it."

"Me, neither." He yawned. "More coffee?"

"Yes, please." Melody closed her eyes and

stretched, her back arching as she reached her fingertips toward the ceiling. She let out a slow, luxurious yawn, her full, hot-pink lips forming in an *O*. Try as he might, Mark couldn't look away. Melody Orlean possessed the uncanny ability to make normal, everyday actions seem sexier somehow.

Professional, Fox. Keep it professional.

Jade and Ty huddled together in the corner, busy editing a segment that was due in the morning. After much consideration and insistence from the Bay News 9 viewers, Mark's producer requested Jade send in a video featuring him skimboarding in the storm.

Filming his dangerous antics seemed like a good idea at first, but now as he considered Melody's words, Mark regretted agreeing to letting them use the footage. He never really considered how reckless his actions might look and that he might be promoting unsafe activities during a storm. All Mark was concerned with was pleasing his viewers and having a good time. While the shots Jade filmed were admittedly pretty good, now, in hindsight, Mark wished he never found the skimboard in the Mali Kai gift shop, after all.

Mark returned to the table he and Melody used to set up their various laptops and devices with two black cups of coffee. For the last five hours, he and Melody worked side by side to track new storm developments, exchange notes, and see what other meteorologists were saying about the hurricane. Even though Mark was typically used to working alone, he could admit it was nice to have someone as smart as Melody by his side, even if she did still make him a little nervous. Mark extended a cup of coffee in her direction. "It's gonna be a long night."

"Thanks." She accepted the steaming beverage. "Looks that way."

Mark sucked in a lung full of air, steeling himself for the question that continued to tug at his heart and his ego. Ever since their communal candlelight dinner, the topic of exactly *why* Melody had a problem with him and what he could have done to make her mad so long ago burned deep in his chest. She wasn't offering up a reason for her unexplained annoyance, and between that and her very presence torturing his libido, he could only stand so much. He needed to know. Mark leaned over and rested his elbows on his knees. "So, are you ever going to tell me what I did to make you hate my ever-loving guts?"

Melody sputtered and choked on her coffee. She scrambled to cover her mouth and met his gaze with wide eyes. She sat straight and dabbed at the corner of her mouth with a napkin. "I don't *hate your guts*." She forced out a laugh. "That would be childish. Ridiculous."

"Well, you're certainly not a fan." Mark leaned way back in his chair and folded his hands behind his head. He stared across the table with tired, heavy eyelids and tried not to smile. Even at this late hour, she still looked fresh and awake, and every bit as lovely as the first day she stormed into his live shot.

Melody cleared her throat and took another sip of coffee, then rested her chin in her hand.

Her expression was thoughtful and faraway. Mark didn't know if he wanted an answer to his question after all, or if he just didn't like the idea of someone not liking him. Either way, the more time he spent stuck in the hotel with Melody, the more he realized he most definitely didn't want her to hate him.

After another beat, she rested her forearms on the table in front of her and leaned forward. "You really don't remember anything from college?"

Mark shook his head, leaning in to match her posture. They were so close now that he could smell the lavender scent of her hair again and count the freckles on the bridge of her nose. They were the closest they had been to each other the entire weekend, with the exception of bashing into each other's foreheads. "I remember you yelling an expletive at me right after graduation. But I had no idea why."

Melody shifted in her seat and stared into her coffee cup. "That was not one of my finest moments. Sorry about that."

"Well, I'm pretty sure I can forgive you if I know what I did to deserve an f-bomb." He smiled.

Melody placed her coffee cup on the table, her features set and serious. "I was in the running for the only internship at Bay News 9 that summer after we graduated. The head producer at the time pretty much assured me that I would get it."

"James." Mark steepled his fingers under his chin. "He retired last year."

"Well, the morning of graduation I called one more time to make sure." A low, deep chuckle escaping her throat. "Up until that point, everything was set for me to start the internship, and I just needed the final confirmation. But when I spoke to James that morning, he apologized and told me the position had been filled."

Mark blinked. The rusty cogs of his memory screeched back to life.

"Imagine my reaction when Jeremy Waits told me

you were bragging to the entire graduating journalism class about your internship." She shrugged. "And how the only reason you got it was because your father was friends with the editor, *James*."

Mark exhaled and looked over at the Doppler radar on her computer screen, trying hard to rest his gaze anywhere but at Melody. The big blob that was Hurricane Lorraine continued to crawl toward them. At that moment, he wanted the hurricane to hurry and make landfall already. Perhaps, if he was lucky, the eye of the hurricane would suck him up and carry him out to sea. "Yeah, I was kind of thoughtless back then." The heat in his ears told him that his face would soon be red. "Melody, I had no idea that James already promised the internship to you."

"Well, I realize that now." Melody was still staring out the conference room door.

Mark folded his arms across his chest.

She met his gaze for a moment, then pursed her lips and stared at the floor again. "So that's the reason, I guess. I was invisible to you in college, yet somehow you still managed to affect the course of my life. I know I should have let this go a long time ago. I don't know why I couldn't."

"I made you feel invisible?" Mark's neck itched. His entire body was reacting to the sudden flood of shame and regret. Melody's bright pink lips screwed into a sort of half smile, half frown as she lifted her chin and looked him dead in the eye.

"I suppose a lot of people made me feel invisible back then." She cringed, her forehead and eyes lined. "It's just…it seemed as though you were friendly with everyone in our journalism program. I felt excluded for some reason."

Mark laughed through his nose as he tried in vain to calm himself. Most of his memories from college were lost in the recesses of his mind. Too much partying, too many benders, and too many hungover eight a.m. classes wiped his memory, though old girlfriends from that time were happy to remind him of the stupid things he did. Mark cleaned up his act since then, but his careless and privileged college days were still an embarrassing part of his life in hindsight. "Well, for what it's worth, I don't remember many other people from our graduating class either," he said. "And as for the internship...honestly, I think you dodged a bullet. I'm stuck there now, and I hate it."

"You do?"

"Yeah. I'm trapped. You were better off, I promise. You've been able to work all over the place. Heck, you even got an interview with The Weather Channel!"

"Well, not without clawing my way up the ladder." Melody sighed. "You really don't like being Bay News 9's golden weather boy?"

Mark shook his head.

"But everyone loves you." Melody frowned. "I'm pretty sure there's a Mark Fox fan club on every single social media site."

"Only one. That group has been inactive since last summer." He offered a sideways smirk. "So you know about my fan club, huh?"

A flash of heat crept into her cheeks. "We meteorologists keep tabs on each other, right? Gotta see what the competition is doing at all times to stay ahead."

"I don't think of you as my competition." Mark

laced his fingers together. "We're a team now, thanks to this wild storm."

Melody sat back in her seat and, for the first time, offered an expression that wasn't pinched with anger or furrowed with skepticism. Her eyes were warm and soft, her shoulders were rounded and her full lips were set in a sweet, easy smile. Maybe there was hope for him, after all.

"Okay, *partner*." Melody finished her cup of coffee, a hint of sparkle at the corner of her eyes. She returned to her laptop keyboard and met his gaze, but only for a moment. "Let's get to work on our morning forecasts then. Together."

****

The outer bands of Hurricane Lorraine lashed at the Fort Myers Beach coastline overnight, bringing the intense winds and rain that were expected. Mark stood on the grand balcony with his cup of coffee at hand, dressed in a poncho and his new favorite, neon floral swim trunks overlooking the shoreline, his forehead lined with worry. He spent most of the night watching with interest as the sea edged its way toward the hotel. It was almost 4:00 a.m., and Russel never returned his calls requesting the group move their accommodations to the second floor to avoid the possibility of a flood. If they didn't act fast, everyone was likely to be standing in water at breakfast.

As he and Melody projected, the storm leveled up to a Category 4 hurricane overnight, with winds clocking in at over 120 miles per hour. If Hurricane Lorraine stayed on its course, by eight o'clock that night, the eye would be making landfall on Fort Myers Beach as a Category 5. Melody, Ty and Jade all managed to settle in for a nap, but Mark couldn't sleep. He enjoyed the solace of the stormy night and wanted to keep watch in case of any new developments when it came to the storm. And, boy, was there ever a new development.

Mark turned from the grand balcony and reentered the dark and empty hotel as an eerie vision flashed before his eyes. He could picture the tropical-themed lobby flooded with seawater, the rattan furniture and potted plants bobbing in the choppy water, and the stairwell partially submerged from saltwater brought in from the storm. Mark knew he needed to find Russel and wake up the crew in the conference room ASAP before everyone found themselves in a dangerous situation. For the first time in his career covering hurricanes, Mark Fox would be trapped by the very storm he was covering.

With his pulse thudding in his temples, Mark sped through the lobby to the security guard station where he prayed Russel would still be. Russel was the one and only hotel employee who stayed for the duration of the storm, and Mark hoped the security guard was getting paid quadruple overtime for the gig. As he approached the darkened station, for a moment, Mark was worried he bailed and left them to fend for themselves.

Fortunately, Russel was content and snoozing in his same padded rolling chair, his feet propped up on the main control center desk.

"Hey, Russ!" Mark reached out and gave his massive shoulders a shake.

Russel snorted and moaned.

Two huge, meaty fists balled in the air and flailed in his face. Mark jumped back and lifted his palms in self-defense at the burly, wheezing security guard.

"Bro, you scared me half to death." He wiped the sleep from his eyes. "What's up?"

Mark exhaled, relieved Russel didn't pound his face, but he was still on edge. They needed to hurry and move everyone, and fast. "Russ, I need your help, man." Mark huffed, breathless. "We have a *big* problem."

Chapter Thirteen

"Ty, don't forget the emergency tote!" Melody's anxiety was ratcheted up to eleven as she and the rest of the hurricane crew hustled to collect their things and move. The conference room carpet squished beneath her feet, already soaked in a quarter inch of sea water as she raced against the clock. Standing water was *bad*, and the longer she spent with her feet planted in an electrical conduit, the more her panic manifested.

"What room did Russ say we could use?" Jade slung a laptop bag over her shoulder.

"Rooms 201-204." Mark lugged his cooler behind him. "They should be open."

"Good thing you woke us up when you did." Ty stood and glanced around the room, his camera perched on his shoulder like always. "This storm surge is coming in fast."

"Do you think we'll be able to set up in time for the 6:00 a.m. forecast?" Melody tiptoed through the soggy carpet and out into the hotel lobby.

"I don't know." Ty shrugged. "Maybe we should make the flooded hotel lobby part of our segment?"

Melody paused. That wasn't such a bad idea. Though, the approaching storm surge sent a shiver of terror through her entire body. The drama of a flooded hotel lobby would provide an excellent illustration for the public of exactly why it was important to evacuate as soon as possible before the storm.

Jade and Mark pushed past on the stairs as they hauled bags of equipment and gear to the second floor in a flurry.

Melody looked at the time on her phone and then out the picture window of the Mali Kai lobby as the wind and rain continued to lash against the supposedly hurricane-resistant panes of glass. She prayed the hotel manager was telling the truth about the stability of those window panes. "Okay, let me just check my makeup. We can film our segment on the staircase. That's about as close as I want to get."

"Meet you back here in five?" Ty grimaced.

"You got it." Melody continued up the staircase until she reached the second-floor landing of the hotel. As she searched the numbers on the doors, memories of beachy, high school, spring break parties came flooding back.

The doors to rooms 201 through 204 were open, with Jade unloading her things into room 201 and Mark unpacking in room 203.

Ty turned into room 202.

Before Melody could protest, she realized she would be in room 204 all the way at the end of that wing of the hotel. Room 204 was, of course, the very room that joined directly next to the one Mark was unpacking his things into. She checked her watch again. She didn't have time to worry about room logistics.

Melody tossed her tote bag on the queen-sized bed and surveyed the space. The hotel rooms appeared similar to the way she remembered them from some twenty years ago, with the exception of an upgraded television and modern bathroom fixtures. The decor and furniture hadn't changed at all from the faux bamboo dresser, nightstands, and mirror to the rattan headboard set against a teal wall. The carpet was the same Polynesian print rug that ran throughout the entire downstairs area of the hotel only with a worn path around the bed. The bedspread and matching curtains were also similar to what she remembered—a jungle of lush green tropical foliage and colorful flowers in a kitschy, mid-century print. Even the enormous industrial air-conditioning unit next to the glass sliding door looked the same.

As she slicked her hair into an elastic band and stuffed her ponytail into a WINK News baseball cap, Melody checked her banged forehead in the mirror. Her bruise had faded and could now be fully concealed with makeup, much to her relief. She touched up her lipstick and tucked her blue-and-white WINK News T-shirt into her jeans as she eyed the door separating her room from Mark's.

Melody could hear Mark and Jade clear as day on the other side of the thin walls as he practiced reporting their 6:00 a.m. segment from his room balcony. She checked her reflection one last time as something hard slapped against her own glass double doors. Melody gasped and held a hand to her chest as she closed her eyes and remembered the windows were impact-resistant. She would be fine. The thought occurred for a moment that maybe she *wasn't* any more safe on the second floor of the hotel than in the flooded conference room. Regardless, it was too late now for any of them to bail anyway. Hurricane Lorraine would meet them soon.

With her shoulders back and her mind set on

reporting safety advice and informative facts to the public, Melody left room 204 in a daze. She was rattled by the events of the morning but determined not to let the setbacks stop her from bringing important information to her viewers so they wouldn't be stuck in standing water themselves. She rehearsed her forecast and strode along the second floor hallway of the Mali Kai to shoot her first weather segment of the day. It would be smooth sailing if she could only stop internally obsessing about Mark Fox for the remainder of the storm.

****

"Storm surge predictions now show we could be seeing more than ten feet of flooding in areas along the coastline. As you can see, the lobby of the Mali Kai is already beginning to take on water, and Hurricane Lorraine isn't even scheduled to make landfall until sometime this evening."

Melody swallowed hard as Ty gave her the signal to wrap things up. She was running out of time and didn't get the chance to go through her safety checklist or to warn her viewers of flash floods. Her next weather report was in an hour, but still, she worried the public wasn't taking the storm seriously enough. "Until then, please make sure your homes and pets are secure. We'll be checking back with you on the hour, every hour to bring you exclusive on-scene coverage of Hurricane Lorraine. Reporting live from the Mali Kai resort at Fort Myers Beach, I'm Melody Orlean."

"And, cut." Ty lowered his camera.

"Did we get everything out of the conference room?" Melody asked.

"I think so."

"Thank you. I might ask Jade to switch rooms with me." Melody winced and placed a hand to her brow. "Where is Russ staying, by the way?"

"Jade and I are sharing a room," Ty said. "Russ took 201. Jade and I thought it would be better to bunk together to create a secure control station for all of our gear."

"Oh." Melody pursed her lips. "That's actually a good idea."

"Why? Did you want to switch with us?" Ty stomped toward the stairs.

"It's not a big deal." Melody took one last look at the hotel lobby from above. The sandbags Russel used to secure the front and back glass doors weren't very effective. A full inch of water was now sloshing all around the lobby, and Melody was beginning to suspect the Mali Kai wasn't as hurricane ready as her producer led them to believe. As if to punctuate the situation, a set of fliers and brochures advertising all of the fun things to do in Fort Myers Beach floated through the lobby and down the hall toward the conference room.

Ty turned and threw a pursed-lip expression over his shoulder. "It's Mark, isn't it?"

Melody stopped dead in her tracks. "What do you mean by that?"

"Oh, nothing." Ty chuckled in a singsong voice, his lips curled in a smile. "Just that if you two don't hurry and hook up, I think the roof of this hotel might blow off."

"*Tyson Pierce!*" Melody smirked and gave his arm a light, playful smack. "That is *completely* inappropriate."

"*Okay.*" Ty rolled his eyes.

"Why? Did Mark say something?" Melody edged closer and whispered as they passed room 202.

"See? I told you." Ty smiled.

"Okay," Melody huffed. "Fine. *Yes*, he is driving me insane in more ways than one. But I am a professional. I think I can manage sharing a wall for one more night."

"Well, maybe it's a good thing that you two have to share connected rooms then." Ty leaned on the door frame of room 202. "Y'all can finally work out whatever this is between you."

"Nobody is hooking up with anybody," she whispered.

Ty smirked and disappeared into the room. "We'll see about that."

"See about what?" Jade appeared behind Melody.

"Nothing." Melody hissed.

Ty flopped on the bed and cackled to himself. "I was just telling Melody that she and Mark need to kiss and make up." He let out one last whoop of laughter and sat up.

"Oh yeah, you two totally need to make out." Jade took a seat at the rattan desk. "You could cut the sexual tension between you with a butter knife."

"I'm leaving now." Melody covered her ears. "I'm going to pretend I didn't hear that!" With her hands still clamped over her ears, she turned onto the second floor hallway with her gaze trained to the floor. Her ears burned beneath her fingertips as she blocked out the playful taunts and teases from the weather crew.

Make out. She scoffed, shaking her head. *How childish!*

Their playful mocking brought back waves of

middle school shame in an odd, nostalgic sort of way. They weren't wrong, though. As she turned out of the room, Melody lifted her gaze from the colorful carpet barely in time to avoid colliding with Mark Fox once again. "Mark." she screeched much louder than she would have liked.

"Ooh, sorry." He steadied himself and grabbed her by the shoulders.

The palms of his hands were on fire, even through the thick cotton material of her work shirt. Hot and *strong*.

"We gotta stop running into each other like this."

A low, nervous giggle escaped from Melody's lips as she stared at the patterned carpet again. For once, she was speechless.

"Your forehead bruise looks better." Mark lifted his gaze to match hers.

"Yours, too. Hey, thanks again for moving so fast to get us up here."

"Yeah. We're a team, right?"

"Right." Melody nodded. "I think I'll lie down for a bit."

"Catch ya later then."

Melody's cheeks were hot to the touch, as if she spent the day out in the sun. She retreated to room 204 and dove into the tropical rainforest print bed. The embarrassing feeling of nostalgia and something she couldn't quite place hit hard as she buried her face into the scratchy bedspread. *Middle school.*

At thirty-eight, Melody knew she was far too old to be gushing and mooning over a man the way she was. She was far too tired for romance anyway after her recent divorce. She worked hard to build up her emotional wall and wasn't interested in letting some good-looking meteorologist from her past tear it down. Still, she couldn't deny Mark Fox had a unique way of making her temperature and pulse elevate. Boyish good looks? Check. Knowledgeable and passionate about the weather? Check. Good in the kitchen? Check. Good in bed? Remains to be seen. *Won't* be seen. Not while she was still on assignment, that is.

Still, as Melody lay in her lonely hotel room trying *not* to think about Mark Fox, Hurricane Lorraine continued to pick up intensity outside. The storm shifted and churned across the earth, roaring and building speed, as if echoing something that was stirring inside her own heart. The idea that the only thing separating her and Mark from being completely alone together in a quirky hotel room was a tiny latch and the turn of a knob was too much to bear. As she closed her eyes and willed Mark, his bare chest, and sea-colored eyes from her mind, the wind continued to howl and blow, bringing the eye of the storm ever near.

Chapter Fourteen

"She likes you, dude." Jade laid out a royal flush as a low, cackle escaped from her throat.

Mark exhaled in defeat, blowing a blue plume of cigar smoke out the cracked balcony sliding door.

Jade gloated and danced in her chair.

"Cheater." Mark smirked and shook his head.

"I won fair and square, and you know it." Jade clapped. She scooped up the jackpot of cash in the center of the table and took stock of her winnings. The pile contained about twenty dollars in quarters, but with the Mali Kai second floor vending machine as their only food source for the foreseeable future, it was an excellent win.

"I got distracted." Mark fingered his cards. "What do you mean? Who likes me?"

"Melody, man." Ty tossed his hand on the table. "You were saying how she hates you, but I can tell from experience that she really doesn't."

"It's so obvious." Jade shook her head and stacked quarters.

Mark blinked and rubbed at the fading bruise on his forehead. "She's just tolerating me."

"You straight people are the worst." Ty laughed. "Stubborn and childish."

"Hey! I'm trying to be a professional here." Mark dealt out another hand. "We're *working*. She doesn't want some jerk she knew in college to put the moves on her in the middle of a hurricane."

"He's got a point there." Jade smiled and counted her winnings.

"Okay, but if you both are into it, if you both *consent,* then there's no problem." Ty shrugged.

"I just don't want to look like a creep any more than I already do." Mark rearranged the cards in his hands. "Jade, help me out here."

"Don't look at me for too much advice." Jade shrugged. "I'm not into relationships. Period."

The entire crew had been awake for almost twenty-four hours, stuck in the hotel and desperate for sleep or some kind of release. Even though they still needed to check in for hourly live storm updates as the storm gained intensity and grew ever near. A gust of wind blew through the crack in the hotel door, bringing a blast of rain.

Mark shut the glass sliding door against the howling storm and put out his cigar. It would be time for his final 6:00 p.m. report on the balcony, anyway. The hurricane was now a certified Category 5, and it would simply be too dangerous to film outside in his usual weatherman-getting-battered-by-the-wind-and-rain shtick. Soon, everyone in the hotel would have to take cover for a while and the only filming they could do had to be inside. It was going to be a heck of a ride, and Mark was ready.

As Mark was getting ready to start up another round of poker, their game was interrupted by three sharp raps on the door that separated his room from room 204.

Jade and Ty both shared a knowing look over their

cards.

Mark rose to answer the knock, checking his hair in the mirror over the dresser before he answered.

On the other side of the door, to no one's surprise, was a slightly annoyed-looking Melody Orlean. She managed a smile and glanced past Mark to the table brimming with playing cards, coins, snacks, and empty beer bottles. "What are you guys up to?"

"Poker." Mark's eyes grew wider at the sight of her. He hadn't seen her since they moved into the adjoined hotel rooms, each of them busy working on their various hurricane update segments and napping in between. "Wanna join us?"

"Is that cigar smoke I smell?" Melody wiggled her nose.

"Oh, yeah." Mark cringed. "It's a smoking room. I cracked the window. Is it bothering you?"

"I didn't even know hotels still had smoking rooms." Melody's face scrunched up, and her entire body trembled as she released a loud sneeze into the sleeve of her hoodie. "I can smell it in my room, that's all. I think it's coming through the crack in the door."

"Sorry. I put it out. If it's bothering you, I won't do it again."

"Thanks." Melody sniffed. "Well, enjoy your game. Sorry I interrupted." She waved and closed the door behind her, sealing the passage between their rooms with the click of the chain latch on the other side.

Mark looked over at Ty, who was already sharing another knowing smile with Jade. "What?" Mark threw down his hand.

"See?" Jade shrugged. "She likes you."

"She tolerates me." His eyes rolled up to the

ceiling. Still the thought continued to percolate in the back of his mind. What if he was wrong?

****

Despite being consumed by Melody Orlean and Hurricane Lorraine, the effects of the cigar combined with a late-morning beer made Mark sleepy. He dozed after his midday report, regaining consciousness long enough for his 1:00 p.m. on-air regurgitation of the same information as before. Hurricane Lorraine was moving at a slow and steady pace, but the water level in the hotel lobby continued to rise. By 2:00 p.m., Mark and Jade were reporting on the two feet of seawater that seeped into the Mali Kai lobby. Little by little, he became more and more unsure of whether the kitschy, old beach hotel would hold up during the storm. "Hey, Russ, you got a minute?" Mark tapped on the door of room 201 where the security guard kept a low profile. Like them, his energy was running on low due to lack of sleep and high anxiety.

After a few heavy footsteps hit the floor, a gruff and grumpy Russel opened the hotel room door, wearing only a T-shirt and boxers. "What's up?"

"Oh, sorry." Mark started at the ceiling. "I wanted to double-check on our generators. You know, since we moved up here, I wanted to make sure they were secure, and we wouldn't lose power."

"Yeah, I got them set up on level three." Russ flexed and rolled his shoulders. "Should be fine."

"Great." Mark tried to look everywhere but directly at Russ and his massive, intimidating frame. "Well, sorry I bothered you."

"Hey, man, while you're here…what do you know about that Melody Orlean chick?"

Mark blinked and met Russel's stare as the security guard leaned up against the door frame. He was a true specimen of a human and, by Mark's estimation, probably clocked in at around three hundred pounds of pure muscle, hair, and testosterone. The term "Alpha Male" floated through his thoughts as he struggled to keep a straight expression. "Um, not much. Why?"

"She married?" Russ scratched the back of his head.

One of his massive biceps popped into his line of sight. "Don't think so." Mark shook his head, lips pursed.

"Got any kids?"

"I didn't ask."

"Well, I'm gonna find out once I'm off the clock." Russ lifted his gigantic arms over his head. He stretched and yawned before looking out the door down the hallway and then back at Mark. His dark eyes scanned the weatherman in his poncho and colorful floral swim shorts. "You two a thing or something?"

"No," Mark blurted, almost too loud. "I mean, I'm *working*."

"Good." Russel smiled and stared into the hall again.

A sick sort of feeling edged into Mark's gut as he fully regarded the expression on Russel's face. Jealousy and disgust flooded through his veins at the image of Russel pawing at Melody like some sort of brute. Protecting his fellow meteorologist wasn't his job or his place. In fact, he could sense that she would tell him she could handle herself. But at that moment, something clicked inside Mark. The idea of losing his chance with her to Russ lit a fire underneath him. A fire that was already smoldering. "Well, thanks for keeping us safe, chief." Mark nodded. "I'm gonna head back. Got a storm to track and all."

"Okay." Russel yawned. "Wake me if you need anything."

With that, the door to room 201 closed, and Mark let out a sigh of relief. He scoffed to himself as the thought of Melody and the beefy security guard together caused a pit to well up in the center of his chest. *Russel. She wouldn't be interested in a guy like him. Would she?*

The idea of the meaty security guard pawing at Melody continued to haunt Mark as he returned to his room, his initial wave of sick jealousy turning into frustrated anger. Part of Mark wanted to warn Melody of the oncoming advances of the hotel security guard; it would be the right thing to do. Another part of him wanted to come out and tell her that he was interested in her himself. Too many variables were in play. The time wasn't right, and Mark had too many strikes against him.

He liked Melody Orlean. He *more* than liked her, and Mark knew he needed to play his cards right if he didn't want to screw up his chances. He needed to play it cool and be respectable. Show her he wasn't the jerk she remembered from college. Still, with Melody on the other side of the door and a literal wolf right down the hall, the urge to blurt out his feelings ached beneath the surface.

Mark walked to their shared door and held his fist high, then pulled back again. He wasn't going to do it. *No.* In twenty-four hours, Hurricane Lorraine would have done her worst to the Gulf Coast, and they would all be headed back home. Mark could deal with this thing he was feeling for Melody then. It would be the professional thing to do.

Just as he was about to go bury his head under a pillow, a knock at the shared hotel room door spiked Mark's sense of hope. He jumped back and undid the turn lock on his side of the door. His door flung open, bringing with it a breeze of lavender and eucalyptus.

"Mark." Melody's lips pouted into an *O* shape as they met each other's gaze.

He breathed in a deep lungful of her heavenly aroma as he scanned over the woman at his door, a vision of curves and pure feminine power. She showered and changed out of her typical work outfit into another body-hugging wrap dress, this one almost the same color as her lipstick. He was so happy to see her, so enchanted by hearing his name on her lips and seeing her wild, damp hair tumbling in curls around her shoulders that he almost forgot himself. Mark blinked and snapped himself out of the scenario that instantly manifested in his sexually frustrated mind. "What's up?" His voice was high and tight. He cleared his throat.

"There's something I need to show you." Melody grabbed his hand and yanked him through the doorway.

For a split second, Mark thought his daydream fantasy might be coming true. But it was like Ty said, if the relationship is consensual, then it's fine. And at that moment, she was pulling *him* into *her* room, and Mark absolutely 100 percent consented. "Melody, are you sure?" Mark asked, a drugged, almost goofy smile plastered across his face. "Here? Now?" His enthusiasm deflated as she pulled him past the bed and toward the double glass sliding doors.

"Huh?" She dropped his hand, her face contorted in an expression of pure confusion.

With every passing second, it became more and more clear she was not inviting him in for a no-strings-attached quickie.

Melody pointed out the window toward the Gulf of Mexico, which was now crashing right up against the back door of the hotel.

Bobbing along in the water and being battered by the thrashing waves was Jade's half crushed Bay News 9 work van being washed out to sea.

Melody turned back and placed a hand on Mark's shoulder.

He stared gape-mouthed at the scene that unfolded before their eyes. Hurricane Lorraine continued to scream outside, almost as loud as the scream Mark was suppressing deep inside.

Melody stared back, her usually flushed complexion devoid of all color. "We've got a big problem."

Mark nodded back and glanced at Melody's hand, soft and delicate on his shoulder. He swallowed, his heart pumping wildly in his ears. "Yep. A *really* big problem."

Chapter Fifteen

Melody gazed at the storm-battered Gulf of Mexico as the lights flickered in her hotel room all around her. In a little less than two hours, Hurricane Lorraine was scheduled to make landfall on Fort Myers Beach as a Category 5 storm. For the last two hours, she huddled into room 202 with Ty, Jade, and Mark going over the latest spaghetti models and storm graphs, but nothing changed. The hurricane was staying on course, meaning over the next five to six hours, all of Lee County would be pummeled with winds in excess of 170 miles per hour, leaving a wake of devastation in its path. Everything in her hometown would be destroyed, including the neighborhood where her mother and brother lived. "*Ma.*" She cradled the phone between her shoulder and her ear. "Everything okay?"

Her mother only sobbed on the other line.

She squeezed her eyes shut. Melody hoped that hearing her mother's voice would help, but calling home only made her feel worse. Guilt wracked its way through her as she stayed on the line, helpless as her mother cried in her ear. She should be home with her family, not waiting this storm out in some crummy old beach hotel. "Can you put Austin on?" She struggled to listen through her mother's incoherent words. "I love you."

After a moment, the faint voice of her younger

brother could be heard calming their mother. Something slapped against the side of the hotel, making a hard, metallic crunching sound.

"Hullo."

Austin's staticky voice rang in her ear. "Did Ma take her medicine?" Melody winced and chewed her thumbnail.

"Yeah, she just did. I think she'll calm down soon." Austin's voice sounded muffled through the receiver. "What should I tell her?"

"Nothing yet. I don't want her to worry." Melody swallowed the lump that rose in her throat. "I would get that twin mattress from the spare room and put it in the hall bathroom. You know what to do if you hear a sound like a train?"

"Don't worry, I got my bug out plan ready." He murmured something to their mother. "You doin' okay out on the beach?"

"I'm holding on."

"I saw your report about the hotel flooding. I didn't show it to Ma."

"Thanks." She scoffed. "We're all on the second floor now. We should be fine."

"Let me know if I need to come rescue you with the kayak." Austin chuckled.

A moment of silence fell on the line as Melody continued to stare out at the stormy late afternoon.

"Just how bad is this storm gonna be?"

"Worse than Charley, probably. Worse than Katrina. Definitely worse than Andrew." Melody sighed. "I don't know. Just, please, around five o'clock start paying close attention. It's supposed to make landfall sometime around then."

"You got it," Austin said.

"Thanks for being there for Mom." A pang of guilt hit her in the chest.

"Thanks for being there for everyone else. The Mackeys and the Giraldi family weren't planning to board up their windows until I showed them your news report."

Melody half-smiled into the phone. "Thanks. I'll be by as soon as I can, once this thing passes over."

"Peace out, weather nerd."

"*Bye.*" Melody cradled her phone in her hand and glanced at the door that separated her room from Mark's. She sensed herself becoming more and more self-conscious around him as the hours passed. Whether it was due to their forced proximity, shared experiences, or physical attraction, sharing the same room with Mark Fox was proving difficult. She enjoyed a few casual flings since her divorce was finalized; dinner dates from singles' websites that all proved to be underwhelming. However, whatever this new thing that was growing and taking up space between her and Mark, she couldn't deny it felt good. Being around him was exhilarating. The anticipation of meeting him face-to-face around every corner thrilled her. For the first time in a long time, Melody almost felt… happy.

The crew was scheduled to meet for one last meal prior to the hurricane making landfall. The can of black beans and yellow rice would make a meager but sufficient dinner for the crew. Ty had graciously offered to cook the yellow rice on a hot plate in his shared control station of a room with Jade so they could all discuss their final shots for the evening and storm predictions. It was a fun and cozy little way for them to get together. She was getting sick of eating yogurt, fruit, and stale pretzels from the vending machine anyway and loved hanging out with Ty and Jade. The only thing that made her nervous was Mark.

Melody knew she didn't *have* to knock on Mark's door to see if he would be joining them for dinner. But she wanted to. With a fresh application of lipstick and a fluff of her hair, Melody sucked in her stomach, straightened her shoulders, and held a balled fist to the door. She bit her lip and pulled back her hand, ready with a speech, but then thought better of herself. She lowered her fist. *Of course* he would be coming to dinner.

A loud thud reverberated from the other side of the wall, followed by the sound of breaking glass and a muffled "ow." Melody's panic spiked, and memories of long ago came flooding back when her original childhood house in Homestead was pummeled by Hurricane Andrew.

Melody banged on the door, not caring if she seemed desperate or ridiculous. Mark was hurt, and if she ignored his cries for help, she would never be able to forgive herself. "Mark, open up! Are you okay?"

Another loud bang shook the wall between their rooms before the lock on the doorknob clicked. Melody stepped back and blinked as the door flew open, followed by a blast of clean soap fragrance and a wall of steam. Backlit by the light of the adjacent bathroom was a very wet, half-naked Mark Fox.

"What's wrong? Did the path of the storm shift?" Melody's lower lip hung open as she registered the fluffy white towel Mark wrapped around his waist. Her lashes fluttered as her gaze traveled up his torso to his

115

toned arms and the tribal tattoo wound around his bicep. She met his stormy gaze as locks of damp golden hair fell into his eyes. "Is everything okay?" Melody forced her gaze up to the ceiling.

"Oh, yeah." He ran his fingers through his crop of hair.

He caught her staring at his arms as he swept his wet locks from his forehead. She couldn't help herself.

"Sorry about that. I'm pretty clumsy. I think I might have broken the towel bar holder."

"Oh, ha ha." She stared hard at the ceiling, her pulse thumping in her ears. "I was worried something happened. Um, I'll let you get dressed."

"Are you going to meet us in 202 for dinner? I snagged one more bottle of wine from the kitchen before the first floor was totally flooded, if you're game."

"Oh." The apples of her cheeks bloomed with heat. "Yeah, that would be nice."

"Okay, cool." He nodded. He gripped his towel around his waist. "See you in there."

She was done for. Melody took a step back, and her ankles wobbled in her flats like a baby giraffe.

Mark closed their door and locked it.

The image of a wet and partially naked Mark Fox would be forever burned into her memory—an image that, before Hurricane Lorraine, she would have *never* considered. Up until a mere forty-eight hours ago, all Melody would have wanted to do to Mark's half-clothed torso was maybe sock him in the gut. Now, as she floated along the second-floor hall in a haze, she couldn't stop obsessing over what was underneath that towel.

****

"So, I said to my sister, 'It's disc golf, not *dis* golf.' The whole time, she thought I was just playing some mini golf game where we make fun of each other." Jade shook her head and finished her glass of wine.

Melody and Ty threw their heads back and laughed.

Mark frowned at them as his gaze darted around the table. "I don't get it." He rose from his seat and poured everyone a fresh glass of wine.

"Dude, you know. *Dis*, like when you disrespect someone?" Ty laughed. "It's a joke."

"Oh." Mark blinked and slapped a hand to his forehead. "I'm slow sometimes."

"It's okay. My sister didn't even know what disc golf was." Jade shrugged.

The wind screamed outside of the double sliding doors in room 202, cutting through the dinner conversation. A loud clatter sounded in the distance, and the table went silent. The hotel room lights flickered overhead, and something large and heavy crashed outside.

"Sounds like the news van smashing up against the tiki bar again." Jade stared into her cup.

"Could be the tin roof to the pool house." Melody rose from her seat. "Ty and I watched as it started to come loose about an hour ago."

"I'm gonna miss that van." Jade sighed and stared wistfully out the window.

With their last supper of beans and rice gone and conditions worsening outside, both crews cleaned up and prepared for the oncoming storm. Their final news segments were due within the hour before they signed off to take cover for the oncoming hurricane. The strobing lights and monstrous sounds of the storm outside made it so none of the inhabitants in room 202 wanted to separate.

"Has anyone checked on Russel lately?" Jade scooped up one last spoonful of rice.

"Yeah." Mark rolled his eyes. "He was snoring right before we started dinner. I went in to invite him, but he was passed out cold."

"Figures." Ty shook his head. "Well, I don't blame him. One security guard for the entire weekend? That ain't right."

"Maybe we should all just stay here as the eye passes over." Melody sipped her glass of wine. "You know. Safety in numbers. Mark, maybe you and I could co-host the final broadcast." She gazed up from her glass to see Mark and Jade exchanging a look. "What's wrong?"

"I…" Mark scratched the top of his head again and looked to his videographer. "Jade?"

Jade made a face at Mark and threw a wadded napkin in his direction. "Our producer told us that we need to make sure our coverage is different from yours," she said. "In fact, she is pressuring us both to make sure our on-air segments, in her words, *sizzle*."

"What?" Melody slammed her plastic cup on the table almost a little too hard. "Why?"

"I told her the situation here and that we're all working together." Mark shifted in his seat, unable to meet her gaze. "She didn't like it. I've been ignoring her, of course. I'm not in competition with you, and I don't care if my producer wants me to be. But us both appearing in the same on-air segment? I'm pretty sure she would have my head."

"Oh." Melody's shoulders slumped. "Well, that's showbiz for ya."

"I know. It's ridiculous." He winced. "I didn't want to tell you."

"No, I get it." Melody straightened her back and glanced at her watch. "Well, I better go get myself ready for the final forecast. We can all still ride out the storm together after we're done though, right?"

"Yes." Ty offered a reassuring squeeze on the hand. "Safety in numbers."

"Cool." Melody nodded. "Well, thanks for the company and the dinner everyone. These next five or six hours are gonna be rough."

"Nah, we'll make it fun." Mark grinned.

Fun.

If only she could fool herself into thinking that was true.

****

"Be back in just a minute!" Melody waved to Ty and prepared a mental checklist of what she wanted to say to her viewers right before the storm. Blood rushed through her veins as she collected her notes and reapplied her makeup for the final hurricane forecast. Debris smacked against the side of the hotel more and more frequently, and it took everything she had not to jump out of her skin at the slightest sound. As she added a final layer of hot-pink lacquer to her lips, Melody could hear Mark banging around in the room next door. She smiled and laughed to herself, realizing that a few days before, all the excessive noise coming from him would have been infuriating. Now, she found his bumbling somehow endearing.

As Melody was getting ready to walk out the door of her hotel room, a sound like a car crash reverberated through the walls of the Mali Kai, followed by a shrieking howl. A screeching banshee of a storm broke into room 203 and brought all the forces of nature. Melody could feel the pressure in the room drop and, with it, her last shred of hope. Her stomach fell to the floor as her senses kicked into gear. She needed to get to her crew and then they would all be safe together. But then the sound of Mark crying out for help on the other side of the wall stopped her dead in her tracks. She raced to the door that separated their rooms and lifted her locking latch to find the doorknob unlocked. Within moments, Melody entered room 203 and was met with a horrifying sight.

The top of a sabal palm tree burst through the double glass sliding doors, its leafy fronds shuddering in the gusting wind. The entire hotel room itself was alive, the storm blowing up the curtains like a skirt over a street grate. Papers flew about the room in their own private dance as a framed aerial photograph of Fort Myers Beach nailed over the desk teetered along the wall. At the center of it all, pinned to the bed by the top of the tree, was a wounded and terrified Mark Fox.

"Mark," she screamed, his name disappearing in the roaring wind. Rain poured in through the jagged window opening, already soaking the carpeted area in front of the sliding doors. Her hair and dress flew all around her, but at that moment, she didn't care. All she knew was that she needed to get Mark out from under the palm tree, and fast.

"Help! It's on my foot!"

Mark's left ankle was buried in a pit of mattress,

his tanned complexion devoid of color. He was stuck under the crown of the tree which came to rest at the edge of the bed, a situation that was both immediate and dire. Melody couldn't begin to guess how heavy the trunk of the tree was, but the weight of it swallowed his entire foot into the pillowtop. If the tree was a few inches taller, or fell a few inches to the right, Mark might be even worse off.

"Give me your hand!" Melody extended her palm in his direction.

Mark grabbed hold and winced as he struggled underneath the crown of the palm tree and off the bed. He pushed with his free leg, letting out a groan.

Melody pulled. They worked together as Hurricane Lorraine blew rain and debris at them.

After a few good pulls, he was freed.

"Hold on!" She looped his arm around her neck for better leverage. A small river of blood trickled down the side of Mark's face from an open cut at his left eye. He was much heavier and more solid than she expected as he limped by her side toward the open door that connected their rooms. Behind them, the wind continued to scream as more glass broke, and a piece of plywood hurled through the opening above the tree.

"We need to get to Ty and Jade!" She eased Mark onto her bed and closed the door on the destroyed hotel room. Loud crunching glass and metallic scraping noises filled the air as her heart slammed against her chest. Hair stuck to her cheek, wet and wild from the wind and rain as she pulled the dresser in front of the shared hotel room door.

The walls of the hotel quaked all around them. Out the window, she could see nothing against the blurred wall of rain. But the sound. That *sound*. It was a sound she knew all too well. The churn and rush of a locomotive hurling down a metallic track, driven by steam and fire. The sound of something huge and powerful. Something that was right outside their door.

"There's no time." Mark shook his head and stood on one leg. "We have to take cover. *Now*."

Melody wound her arm around Mark's waist as they both hurried to the one room where they would be safest. The words she so often spoke to her viewers raced through her own mind as her body worked on pure instinct. Her hurricane safety training kicked in on autopilot. *Find an interior room with no windows. Bring a pillow to cover your head. Duck and hide.*

As the eyewall of Hurricane Lorraine closed in on the Mali Kai resort at Fort Myers Beach, Melody Orlean and Mark Fox took shelter to ride out the storm. They huddled together in the tiny linen closet, watching and listening as the lights flickered under the gap in the door and the glass sliding doors of room 204 shook in their frame. That evening, Mark Fox and Melody Orlean would miss their final storm forecasts for Bay News 9 and WINK News. Hurricane Lorraine arrived on Fort Myers Beach ahead of schedule.

Chapter Sixteen

Mark's ankle throbbed. It didn't hurt as bad as the time he twisted it playing soccer in college; he was probably drunk at the time. This time, he was sober and hiding from the most powerful hurricane that he ever experienced in a tiny closet with the woman who saved his life. The woman he thought about almost non-stop for the last forty-eight hours. The woman who was, at that moment, pressing a towel against the side of his face.

"Is it still bleeding?" Melody inspected his leg, her voice shaking.

They both sucked in ragged breaths and huddled together in the closet, listening to the storm do its worst outside. "I don't think so." Mark pursed his lips, his features pinched. "Ow."

"I'll text Ty and tell him we are sheltering together." The back lighting of the phone illuminated her face in the dark.

Another loud bang on the glass sliding doors made them both jump.

"I guess these windows aren't impact-resistant, after all." Melody scoffed and tapped her phone screen.

"Well, they're supposed to protect against high winds and projectiles, not *fallen trees*." Mark winced again. "Ow."

"Ty texted back.

—*Ok, stay safe.*—

"Jade is with him, and they are sheltering, too." She shoved her phone inside her bra strap.

Mark tried not to notice her cleavage glowing in the dark closet, thanks to the light of the phone. Even in a life-or-death situation, he couldn't help but look. "You saved me." Mark dabbed at the wound near his eye with his fingertips. "I might still be stuck if you didn't come and help."

"Ty or Russel or Jade would have helped you out, too. I just happened to be nearby."

"Well, I'm glad you were." Mark shifted, and their knees brushed together.

Melody didn't move away as their knees and hips touched. "So, what happened? How did the storm suddenly pick up speed?"

"I don't know. I guess we'll miss our final forecast. No one will see this coming."

"Maybe not." Melody pulled out her phone again. "You have your own online hurricane watch channel, right?"

Mark's face flamed in the darkened closet at the mention of his pet project. "Yeah, why?"

"I'll text Ty and tell him that we are live streaming from your channel. He can send out the word to WINK and Bay News 9, and they'll run our footage from there."

Mark launched FoxForecasts only a month before and didn't have much content yet on his independent meteorology channel. He did have quite a few followers though from Bay News 9 viewers who found him. He didn't advertise the channel or his videos, so the fact she knew about it was surprising, and flattering. Mark wanted to kiss Melody several times during their stay at the Mali Kai resort. However, the urge was never greater than at that very moment. "Melody Orlean, you're a genius." He pulled out his phone from his own back pocket. "Can you use the flashlight on your phone to light the closet?"

"Yep. Ty texted back. He's contacting the station."

"Okay, just a sec." Mark found the live feed recording icon on his screen. "Ready?"

Melody nodded. "Ready."

Melody held her phone light and scooted over next to Mark.

He turned his camera out in the self-facing position and tried to balance it in the cramped space. Both of their faces barely fit in the frame of the screen, but he had to admit, he liked the way they looked together.

"Hey, FoxForecasters, this is Mark Fox on scene at the Mali Kai hotel with my fellow meteorologist, Melody Orlean. Hurricane Lorraine has unexpectedly landed an hour before our original forecast at Fort Myers Beach. We expect the eye wall to run in a straight line through Lee County and then hook left up toward the center of the state. If you haven't yet, seek shelter now! Melody, do you have anything to add?"

Melody glanced over with her lips pressed together.

Her eyes shone with an odd mixture of terror and appreciation.

"Thanks, Mark." She picked up after him without missing a beat. "We are currently sheltering in the closet of room 203 at the Mali Kai hotel as the storm rages outside. A palm tree crashed through the glass sliding door in Mark's room and pinned him to the bed, injuring his ankle. He's all right, but we can't stress enough that the situation is life-or-death out there right now."

"We're signing off now to preserve the battery life on our phones, but we'll log back on as soon as we can. Reporting from inside a closet at the Mali Kai hotel, this has been Mark Fox and Melody Orlean with FoxForecast signing off."

They clicked off the light on their phones, and the closet was dark again as the sound of violent wind and rain continued to pummel the hotel. Mark shifted on his injured ankle, trying hard not to complain too much. They were already in such a precarious situation, and he didn't want to worry Melody more.

"Did that live icon say five thousand people were watching your live stream?" Melody blinked at the screen.

Something large bashed against the glass sliding door. Mark and Melody huddled closer together. "I didn't notice." Mark wasn't paying attention to anything at that moment, except for Melody's thigh rubbing against his. He didn't care about viewers or being injured or even the hurricane for one moment.

"That's a lot of subscribers."

"I suppose." Mark shrugged.

Another loud bang echoed through the walls from the direction of Mark's battered hotel room.

"Sounded like furniture, maybe." Melody's damp hair brushed against his face. Her signature fragrance filled his nose. Suddenly his foot didn't hurt so much anymore.

"Mark, I just realized something." She placed a warm hand on his forearm. "We still ended up filming a news forecast together, after all."

"Ha!" He let out a low, nervous giggle. "I guess we did."

A moment of silence fell between them as the wind outside intensified. The walls shook again, and the thunderous sound of a charging train filled the air.

Melody's hand gripped tighter to Mark's forearm, her fingernails digging sharp half-moons into his skin.

"Mark, I'm scared!"

His ears filled with the sound of sirens and crashing glass, crunching metal and endless shrieks. He slid his arms around Melody's waist and buried his face into her lavender and eucalyptus heaven of hair as the eye wall of the storm found them.

Chapter Seventeen

Hurricane Lorraine showed her ugly face and raged over the Mali Kai resort that evening as the Bay News 9 and WINK News crews continued to shelter inside. After what felt like an eternity, a false sense of calm fell over Fort Myers Beach once again. Melody released her grip from around Mark's neck and breathed a sigh of relief as the whooshing gales of wind outside subsided. After almost two hours spent listening to the sounds of crumbling masonry, ripping metal, and sickening thuds, they made it through the first wave of terror.

For the moment, the Mali Kai resort was inside the eye of the storm; a calm and still center where the pale afternoon sun shone as though hurricanes didn't even exist. The last measurement Melody was able to check from her huddled closet shelter showed the eye scaled some thirty miles in diameter, and the storm was moving at around ten miles per hour. In less than thirty minutes, the back half of the eye wall would come to visit them once again.

Mark lifted his head. "Are you okay?"

Melody nodded and opened the closet door out to her room, unsure of what she should expect. Pale light streamed in through the glass sliding door, causing her eyes to blink and readjust after so long in the dark. Her room was still miraculously intact, though the carpet squished beneath her feet. Rainwater seeped in through the crack under the door that separated rooms 203 and 204. She could only imagine what Mark's old hotel room must look like now. "We need to go check on Ty and Jade while we can. Stay put. I'll be right back." Melody left him sitting on her bed as she opened the door to room 204 onto an unexpected sight. Daylight streamed in from the hallway and the second floor hallway was now obstructed with palm fronds, twisted metal, broken glass, soggy drywall, and debris. A giant beam ran through the center of the hall, blocking her path to the main stairs. She leaned her head out the door to see the side of the Sandpiper resort—the Mali Kai's beachfront neighbor—also torn to shreds. The entire north side of the building was ripped away, and a beam from who knows where lodged itself directly in her path to freedom.

Pinpricks of fear ran down her spine as she closed the door, her body sinking as she tiptoed back to the bed. Water flooded over her feet, soaking her shoes. They were trapped, Mark was wounded, and all they could do was wait.

A pale and bloody Mark gazed back with wide eyes. "It's bad out there, isn't it?"

Melody nodded and closed her eyes before finding her voice. "Half of the hotel is gone. We're trapped."

Mark grimaced. He patted the bedspread next to him and motioned for her to take a seat, then took out his phone. "I'll try to call Jade. Hopefully she'll answer."

Melody forced her dead-weight legs to lower her body onto the tropical print comforter. Adrenaline coursed through her veins making her want to run but rendering her unable to move a muscle all at once.

129

Mark's voice sounded far away, even though he was seated right next to her as an overwhelming sensation took hold. Memories of her own home being ripped apart around her as a girl echoed through the recesses of her mind as she floated out and up above herself, detaching from the current situation.

"Melody." Mark caressed her shoulder.

She sucked in a startled breath through her nose. Her chest and shoulders were rigid, but as she looked over at Mark, the world came into focus again. She blinked and sucked in a ragged breath as her heart went *thud-thud-thud* in her ears.

"Ty and Jade are okay. Something is stuck against their door, so they are trapped for now, too. We just need to stay put until the eye wall passes back over again."

"No." She suppressed a gag.

"I think you're going into shock." Mark hobbled back to the closet and opened the door. He patted around on the overhead shelf and searched for an extra blanket. He found a soft waffle knit throw, limped back over to the bed, and wrapped it around her shoulders. "Do you need something to drink? Some water? Anything?"

Melody shook her head. "Thank you." She pulled the satin-edged blanket tighter around her shoulders. "This is bringing back some terrible memories."

"Do you want to talk about it?" He checked his phone again. "We have probably twenty more minutes before we have to go back into the closet."

Melody struggled to even out her breathing as the room tilted ever so slightly. She was coming back down from her panicked state, but not entirely. The old

Melody Orlean would have hated looking so weak in front of Mark. The old Melody Orlean wouldn't have shared the story that she was about to share. But she wasn't the same person anymore. *He* wasn't the same person. Hurricane Lorraine saw to that.

"I was a little girl when Hurricane Andrew came through Homestead." Melody ran her fingers along the satin edge of the thermal blanket, held her breath, and paused for a moment before she began again. "We lived there at the time in a nice little house. I don't remember too much, but I remember my mother's screams. I remember holding on to my little brother Austin for dear life as she used her body to shield us. The roof came off, peeling away just like a child ripping the lid off of a toy."

Mark placed a hand on her shoulder and squeezed. He didn't say a word, only continued to listen.

"The plumbing of the house saved us. My mom held on to the tub and covered us, but I could feel the storm sucking us into the air. We were homeless after that, of course. That's how we ended up living in San Carlos Park, just down the road."

Mark cleared his throat. "That must have been terrifying. No wonder you're so passionate about storm safety."

Melody nodded. "We lost an uncle afterward. My mother's brother. He died of exposure. She hasn't been the same since. So, there it is. My personal vendetta against nature. And nature just won again."

"Nature didn't win. *We* won. We still figured out a way to warn the public. *You* figured out a way to warn the public. You probably helped a lot of people just now."

131

Melody sniffed and looked over at Mark. His face was so kind and understanding at that moment. She could hardly believe she used to want to punch it. "The worst part is, I know the storm is coming for my brother and my mother now, and I can't do anything, I'm trapped. Again."

"My parents moved to New Mexico after I graduated high school." Mark laughed a little through his nose. "I don't have to worry about them being caught in a storm like this. I can't imagine how helpless you must feel."

"That's what I should have done." Melody snorted. "I should have taken that Weather Channel position and moved my mother out of hurricane country. Too late now."

"Can you call or text your family?"

Melody shook her head and pulled her phone out of her bra strap. If she still wasn't in the throes of shock, she might have been embarrassed about where she stashed her phone, but at that moment, she didn't care. "Austin already texted me. He said they are still fine, and it's calm now. I guess he watched our live stream."

"Good." Mark rose from the bed. "I gotta use the restroom. I'll be right back."

Melody nodded as he attempted to put weight on his injured foot.

Mark braced himself on the wall and hopped on one foot, closing the bathroom door behind him. He emerged a few minutes later with his face freshly washed and a bandage over the cut near his eye.

Somehow with his grown-in stubble, unruly hair, and banged-up features, Mark was even more handsome than usual. "You know, this storm-ravaged look suits you." Melody caught his gaze and held it.

He smiled at the floor and ran a hand through his damp locks.

It wasn't fair that he looked so good after being stuck in a storm. "I need to use the restroom while I still can." Her cheeks burned as she rose from her seat. "Be right back." Melody closed the bathroom door behind her and lit the darkened bathroom with her cell phone flashlight. Her reflection in the mirror looked like she suspected it would: dirty, exhausted, and frazzled. Her mass of thick hair was fuller than ever as the humidity caused her natural curl to spring back to life. She relieved herself and washed her hands and face, attempting to look as presentable as possible. Her makeup was on the dresser, but at that point, she didn't care about reapplying her lipstick for the millionth time that weekend.

Mark turned his attention from his phone as she emerged from the bathroom. A nagging realization hit her all over again. Melody was more self-conscious than ever at the idea of being cocooned in the linen closet with her fellow meteorologist for two more stormy hours. The thought of their knees brushing together and their lungs breathing in the same air made her head spin.

Oh no.

Melody cleared her throat and bit her lower lip. She folded her arms across her chest and tried to shake off whatever feeling was manifesting inside of her. "I guess we should take shelter again."

Mark scratched the back of his neck and gave her a side-eyed glance, his mouth set in an easy, steady smile. The term "smoldering" came to mind, but she blinked it away.

"Do you want to ride this one out in the bathroom instead?"

Melody cleared her throat and tried not to blush at the prospect of riding anything out with Mark. The innuendo almost made her mind go blank. "Oh, um…I thought of that." She blushed. "That sliding pocket door doesn't seem so secure though. And the bathroom backs up to the hallway, which is exposed now."

The soft pitter patter of rain on the glass sliding doors signaled the return of Hurricane Lorraine. Mark nodded and rose from the bed.

The calm at the center of the storm was about to pass, and fierce wind speeds would soon be battering the hotel and all of Fort Myers Beach again. This time with much less ceremony and panic, Melody and Mark filed into the little closet that protected them for the first half of the hurricane.

"Ready for round two?"

His perfect weatherman smile shone back in the dark. She wrapped herself in the thermal blanket, grateful for the comfort. Even though she knew from experience the worst was yet to come, Melody was almost hopeful. She pushed through the waves of fright that threatened to overcome her and managed to return his smile with a nod. "You bet." Melody grinned. "Piece of cake."

****

"Should we film another live stream segment?" Mark tapped away at his phone in the dark and responded to his producer as the back eyewall of the storm descended with full force.

Melody's producer also texted to check on them

134

and assured that help would be on the way as soon as travel was safe. However, with reports that all of Fort Myers Beach was underwater with downed power lines, littered highways, and mass damage to the landscape and property all around, help might realistically not be on the way for a very long time. "Yeah, another live stream wouldn't be a bad idea." She nodded. "I'm sure your viewers would like to know that you're doing okay so far."

"And yours, too." Mark flashed his phone screen toward her. The comments section on his last live stream exploded. "You've got quite the fan base on FoxForecasts."

Melody took the phone from his hand and scrolled through the eight hundred comments that populated from their live feed during the storm. Well-wishers and people thanking them for the last-minute update from all over the county made her chest swell. This was it. This was the kind of personalized, up-to-the-minute, storm-chasing information she always wanted to provide to the public. The only problem is that it came at a dangerous cost. "Okay, let's do it." She fluffed her now frizzed, but fully dry hair. "I probably look like a mess, though."

Mark shook his head. "You look great."

Even as she still recovered from shock, the compliment hit her in all the right places. The idea of reporting alongside Mark again filled her chest with a warm, honey-like sensation. Even as Hurricane Lorraine did her best to continue to chip away at the Mali Kai, Melody found herself dealing with her current situation with a clearer head and a more grounded heart. The gripping panic that flooded her system before was now replaced with a cozy energy, and even a blush of optimism. Melody Orlean, meteorologist and environmental hazard champion of the people, was back.

As the patter of rain outside turned to steady machine-gun slaps against the glass sliding door, Melody scooted next to Mark again in the dark, cramped linen closet. She was getting used to feeling his weight at her side and the clean laundry scent of his shirt with just a hint of salt and smoke. She was beginning to crave it.

"You want to lead this time?"

Melody squinted her eyes as he passed her the phone. "You're sure?"

"Yeah. This is your show just as much as mine now. I couldn't do the live feed without you."

Melody's smile screwed up into a strange sort of frown. "Mark Fox, I think that's the nicest thing you've ever said to me." She held the camera out in front of them. They had to huddle close together to get both of their faces into the frame. Melody sucked in a deep breath and steadied her shaking hand as she prepared for their live weather report. "In three, two…This is Melody Orlean reporting from a closet at the Mali Kai resort on Fort Myers Beach with my co-meteorologist Mark Fox. The worst of the storm is yet to come…"

Chapter Eighteen

The back half of Hurricane Lorraine tore through the hotel with winds in excess of 150 miles per hour. The storm did its worst, whipping and screaming from beyond the safety of their shelter. Most of the building was gone, creating even more edges and crevices for the hurricane to sink her windy claws into. For Mark, the terrifying realization the hotel was being ripped apart around them still didn't quite sink in. The sounds of crushed concrete and ripping steel echoed through the walls of the hotel; yet, being trapped in the middle of a disaster wasn't the only thing on his mind.

"Talk to me, Mark." Melody hugged her knees and rocked in place. "I need something to distract me."

Mark glanced at her from his phone. "Okay. Ask me something."

"Anything?"

He nodded. "Anything."

"What really happened between you and Jennifer Green?"

He was glad to talk to Melody to pass the time, but when it came to the subject of relationships, he would rather hurl himself headfirst into the storm. He put his phone aside, let out a deep sigh, and stared up at the closet ceiling. "Okay, anything but that."

"Why?" Melody's golden eyes glittered in the low light.

He wasn't sure how much to give away at this point. However, with death and destruction quite literally at their door, he didn't see much reason to hold back anymore. Keeping his emotions to himself wasn't serving him well up to this point as it was. "Because I think you're starting to not hate me so much. The story of me and Jennifer Green isn't pretty."

"I'll tell you about my divorce." She offered him a thin smile. "That's not a pretty story, either."

Another large crash in the hallway beyond their closet door caused them both to jump. Maybe talking about Jennifer Green wouldn't be worse than death, after all. He closed his eyes and exhaled. "Okay, so I was a bad boyfriend."

"And?"

"And…and I just couldn't give her what she wanted."

"Which was?"

Mark opened his eyes and looked up across the dim closet under a curtain of hair. No one ever asked him about this sort of thing before. Not his parents. Not his coworkers. Especially not his friends. Now, as the world crashed around them, Mark found himself opening to someone he least expected. "She wanted a commitment, and I couldn't give it." He leaned his head on the closet wall with a soft thud.

"That's it? You didn't cheat on her or insult her dog or steal from her or anything?"

"No. But Jenn wasn't the first. Pretty much all my relationships ended over the years for the exact same reason."

"Oh." Melody wrapped her blanket tighter around her shoulders.

A look of what he could only interpret as disappointment caused a burning panic to rise in his throat. "But that doesn't mean I wouldn't ever want to commit to someone."

An uncomfortable silence settled between them as Hurricane Lorraine continued to do her worst outside. Mark's ears burned from his failed and desperate attempt to backpedal out of the conversation.

"I thought my ex was committed to me." Melody's face was illuminated by the backlighting of her phone. "Turns out I was the only one living up to our vows."

Mark scowled and shifted. "I'm sorry to hear that."

"It's okay. At least you can admit it." Melody snorted. "It's better to tell the truth about how you feel than to live a lie."

"I suppose." Mark sat in silence for a moment, mulling over what to say next. The hurricane was draining him, but talking about emotions left him dull and flat. "How much battery life do you have left?"

"Less than ten percent."

Mark groaned. "I'm at five percent. We should reserve our phones for when the rescue crews come around. Recording our live streams zapped my battery."

"Good point." Melody frowned. "I'll power off."

They stashed their devices, and the closet was dark again. Only the sound of their labored breathing and the ravaging winds outside filled the space between them.

Melody tapped on his shin. "How is your foot?"

"Still hurts. I don't think anything is broken though."

"That's good."

Melody's bare knee brushed his again as something loud banged against the glass sliding door. The walls of

139

the hotel shuddered as though a small earthquake was ripping through the foundation, grinding the very floor and walls around them to dust. A smooth, soft hand shot out in the dark and landed on Mark's knee as they both braced for something bad. After a moment, the shaking stopped, but Melody's hand remained in place. Mark didn't mind. "That was scary." He laughed, a strange sort of nervous laugh.

"What did we do wrong, Mark?" Melody panted. Her hand gripped his leg even tighter. "Why didn't we see this coming sooner?"

"We tried our best." He placed his hand over her own. "This isn't anyone's fault."

"Now we're stuck here!" The walls trembled again. Melody squeezed tighter. "Ty and Jade and Russel are stuck here."

"You can't blame yourself!" The roar outside their door was now louder than ever. Melody's breath came in hard and fast in his ear.

"We're going to die," Melody screamed; her entire body leaned into him.

The unmistakable sound of glass breaking filled the air as they reached for each other to brace against the worst. The pressure changed inside the tiny closet, causing Mark's ears to pop as his insides hit the floor. That was the moment he realized the storm had breached the hotel room. The howling wind was louder than ever now, blowing through the crack in between the floor and the door and hurling debris against the walls. Within moments, something heavy slammed up against the closet door, muffling the sound of the hurricane which was now right outside.

"We'll be sucked out!"

Her voice was a shrill alarm in his already ringing ears. Mark could only hold onto her tighter as he fought his own urge to lose control. His heart sank as she whimpered in his ear, a cry so devoid of hope he could barely stand it. Working on instinct, he took her face in his hands. Her cheeks were hot and wet with tears under his palms, and her ragged breaths kissed his neck with every sob. "Listen to me." Their faces hovered so close together in the dark. "Listen to my words."

Another loud bang thundered through the shell of the room as her fingers wound around his back, clawing at his shirt and pulling them ever nearer. Her cheeks were so soft and her hair wild and fragrant in his face. As the world was torn apart around them, all he could think about was her, sweet and soft in his arms. He had faith the closet would protect them. It was their sacred space. If they only held on to each other, everything would be okay. "Everything is going to be okay." His voice was slow and low. They were so close now the tips of their noses grazed. Melody's breath hit his lips in warm, wet sobs as more crunching glass broke through the stormy night.

"Kiss me, Mark." Her soft, hot hands flew to his face. "I need you to."

Something big slammed against the closet door, but Mark didn't notice. He leaned in and kissed her full on the mouth, her quivering, pillowy lips salty with tears. They held onto each other as the hotel tore apart all around them, greedily losing themselves in the moment and blocking out the wind, the rain, the destruction. Hurricane Lorraine raged on as they melted into each other, protected in the cell they created together, an impenetrable force of heat and longing compounded by time. No more hesitation and no more animosity surfaced as their desire helped distract them from fear. He kissed her, and she kissed back until the wind outside didn't howl quite so loudly, and the Mali Kai hotel was at peace once again.

Chapter Nineteen

Try as she might, Melody couldn't look Mark Fox in the eye. The light on her phone showed nearly ten o'clock that night as they attempted to escape from the closet, shell-shocked, exhausted and on-edge. It took all their remaining energy and a good amount of pushing, but they finally wedged the door open enough to release themselves from the confines of their storm shelter. And once they emerged, neither was prepared for the damage that greeted them.

"Well, the third floor is gone." Mark gazed up at the exposed ceiling of wires, ripped up drywall, and twisted plumbing.

The entire scene reminded Melody of a post-apocalyptic movie that she begged her former husband to go see with her. Hopefully they wouldn't have to suffer a zombie invasion or aliens on top of Hurricane Lorraine, too.

All-in-all, the state of room 204 was as to be expected after being ravaged by a storm. One of the glass doors was shattered by some unseen projectile, most likely from one of the many pieces of debris that now littered the room. The queen-sized bed was flipped on its side and pushed against the closet door by the wind, and the tropical print curtains were ripped from the rod. The carpet was soaked through, and as before, the door leading out to the hallway was still blocked.

They were trapped and exposed in the battered Mali Kai hotel room until a rescue team arrived—whenever that would be.

"Help me flip the bed back over." Melody's voice was robotic and stern as she got to work.

Mark limped to the bed and helped her push.

The bed flopped back into its usual position with little effort, helping the room to look somewhat back in order.

"Well, now what?" Mark fell onto the bed.

Melody's feet squished around on the carpet as she paced the room. She texted her brother, but he wasn't responding, and her panic accelerated.

"Hey, everybody alive over there?" The voice echoed over the wall from two rooms away.

Melody was never so happy to hear her cameraman in her entire life. "*Ty.*" She gasped and forgot her phone for a minute. "Ty, we're over here!"

"Jade. Are you okay?" Mark called out into the night.

"We're fine," Jade yelled. "You?"

"We're okay." Melody's voice carried through the night in a choked sob.

"Mel, I called our producer. She says we need to sit tight," Ty yelled. "They'll be here in the morning with rescue boats."

"Okay," Melody yelled back. She pushed against the frog in her throat. "Ty, I'm so happy to hear your voice!"

"What about me?" A deep, gruff voice echoed into the night.

"Russ!" Mark laughed out loud. "You okay, man?"

"Yeah, I'm fine," Russ mumbled. "Storm sucked

out my last two beers, though."

"Aw, man, that's so great!" Mark beamed. "Everyone's okay."

"Not everyone." Melody glanced at her phone. "My brother isn't answering. I'm trying not to worry, but my mind is drifting to all the worst possible places."

"You know, I bet his phone just died. Look at our phones, they're almost dead. Everyone without a generator in Lee County is probably without cell service. And let's not forget that some of the towers might be down."

"Good point." Melody gazed at the sky to avoid eye contact with Mark for a little while longer as she continued to contemplate her current situation. A haze raced overhead as Hurricane Lorraine whisked away the last streaks of puffy gray cloud in her wake. Only a few hours before, a devastating storm was churning in the very sky that hovered over their damaged hotel room.

"Well, it's a good thing the storm knocked the bed on its side, I guess." Mark ran a hand along the comforter. "The mattress stayed dry except for the left side. You'll have somewhere comfortable to sleep tonight."

"That was lucky, I guess." Melody lowered herself onto the bed. "What about you?"

Mark shrugged. "I can figure something out and lay on the floor. Maybe I can use the cushions from the armchair to make a bed or something."

Melody kicked off her wet flats and squished her toes into the rain-soaked carpet, cringing at the mushy, wet sensation. "The floor is too wet. I probably won't sleep tonight, anyway. We can both just sit on the bed until help comes."

"If you're okay with that."

"What else are we gonna do, right?" Melody checked her phone again. "My battery is at eight percent."

"Mine's almost dead, too." Mark sighed.

Melody eased onto the bed, propped herself up on the rattan headboard, and folded her hands in her lap. She continued to do everything and anything to avoid making eye contact with Mark. Even though they spent the last four or five hours trapped in a closet together, now seated next to him on a bed and in the open, Melody was more self-conscious and vulnerable than ever. Not to mention the small matter of their unspoken, stormy kiss that hung heavily in the air.

"So." Mark cleared his throat. He sat and smoothed out the bedspread next to him.

She turned her head and was grateful his features were barely visible in the dark "So." She looked away again.

"Do you…want to talk about what happened back in there?"

"Nope." Melody hugged herself. "Not really."

"Oh."

She closed her eyes, her mouth dry and her head heavy. She could still feel the phantom scruff of his beard on her cheek; his lips pressed so desperately against hers. She couldn't remember how long they held onto each other in that dark, cramped closet. Was it a minute? Ten minutes? Time didn't seem to work the same way during a storm. "We were both scared and vulnerable." She opened her eyes and turned her head away. "It's okay. I know it didn't mean anything."

A sudden movement on the bedspread made Melody gasp. Even in the low moonlight, she could see and sense Mark's hand on the bed next to hers.

He flipped his hand over with his palm extended upward.

Her gaze traveled from his hand to his face. His soft eyes stared back from under a curtain of weather-worn hair.

"It meant something to me."

Her breath hitched. Her body was stiff from protecting itself through the storm and from always protecting itself. Her instinct to guard her heart and her body from everyone—including Mark Fox—arrested her. Melody wanted to take his hand, but her body wouldn't let it happen. She sucked in a tight breath and rose from the bed. "Are you thirsty?"

He curled up his hand and folded his arms across his chest, turned his head away, and stared out the broken glass sliding doors toward the beach. "I guess. Don't use the water from the bathroom sink, though. Even if it works, it's not safe."

"I know *that,*" Melody scoffed. "I had a few bottles of water in my cooler. I need to find them." She stumbled across the room and her feet made ridiculous swamp-like sounds. Melody took her time rummaging through the debris in the dark, moving aside water swollen chunks of drywall, pieces of loose wiring, broken chairs, palm fronds and other unidentifiable debris.

She spied her cooler right where she left it on the floor next to the dresser, unmoved and intact. "Found it." She pulled off the lid and leaned over piles of garbage. Melody pawed through the freezing, melted cooler ice until she found two bottles of water, an apple, and a yogurt. She clutched the food and water to her chest as she balanced over the soggy mess back to the bed. "Apple or yogurt?"

"Just the water, please." His voice was flat, just like his expression.

Melody tossed him a bottle and set the apple and yogurt on the side table. Her chest felt hollow as she eased back into her spot next to a now very distant and quiet Mark Fox. Riding out the hurricane was tough, but spending a night next to his cold front would be almost worse.

"Our live coverage seemed to go over well?" Melody ventured.

"Yeah." He exhaled. "Thanks."

"Is the indie weather channel something you want to expand on?"

Mark sniffed and shifted on the bed. "I guess. I've been wanting to get out of traditional television meteorology for a while now. I'm sick of being a robot on air. I want to do my own thing."

The corner of her mouth turned up in a sad sort of smile. "Me, too. I'm tired of trying to fit this perfect image on air. It's not even what's important to me anymore. I want to raise awareness and enact some social change. Get people to see that big, dangerous storms are more and more common now with global warming. We need to be prepared."

Mark made a sound of agreement but continued to keep a chilly distance with his face and body turned away.

Melody rubbed at the heaviness on her chest as they continued to sit together in silence.

Ty and Jade's laughter carried over the walls and into the night.

A pang of guilt crept into her heart. They were safe and sound for the moment, and now they only needed to sit tight until help arrived in the morning. A long, uncomfortable moment settled in.

"Did I do something wrong?" Mark broke the silence between them.

"No." She hugged herself tighter. "Why do you say that?"

"Well, it's just…" He huffed. "I know we didn't start off on the right foot. I know that we have more important things to worry about right now, but…"

"But what?"

Mark sat upright on the bed and held his head in his hands.

Forty-eight hours ago, Melody would have been satisfied she was the cause of his frustration. Forty-eight hours ago, she wouldn't have a lick of empathy or pity for this man sitting next to her. Now as she stood back and witnessed him struggle, she couldn't help but feel a little bit bad. The wall she built to protect herself was momentarily torn down by Hurricane Lorraine, but now, as Mark was visibly hurting because of her, Melody wasn't so sure she wanted to replace those emotional bricks.

"Look, I don't want to make this weird. We're still working, technically, anyway." Mark crossed his arms at his chest and stared up at the sky. "I just wanted to tell you…you know. What happened in the closet? It was nice."

Melody smiled, and her cheeks heated all over again. Her stiff, guarded shoulders softened. "Just nice?"

Mark lifted his head and lowered his hands.

Her eyes adjusted in the dark, working together with all her senses like a creature of the night. She could see his every outline now, the shape of his shoulders, and the silhouette of his profile. She could sense his heat at her side and hear every move he made. Until that moment, she didn't realize how much she would miss looking at and being around Mark Fox once he went home to Tampa. The thought alone broke her heart.

"It was more than nice." He leaned in toward her. "It was everything that I wanted to happen from the moment you ran down the beach and started yelling."

Melody choked. The words she constantly bit back were threatening to spill out. She couldn't take it anymore. "I always liked you, Mark."

"What?" Mark flinched, and his brows came together, though his lips were fixed in a smile.

"I *did*." She bit her lower lip. "I know you probably don't believe me, but back in college, all I wanted was for you to see me. I wanted you to smile and joke around with me like you did with everyone else. But you didn't, and it hurt. It hurt bad." Melody extended her hand across the comforter with her palm upturned as Mark caught her gaze through the dark of night. With the storm now rumbling far off in the distance and the sky open over their heads, the sound of the waves crashing, their unsteady breathing, and her own heartbeat in her ear combined to create a hypnotic, romantic ambience.

Mark took her hand in his.

The skin-to-skin contact flooded her body with

much-needed endorphins. The world almost completely fell apart around them, but now, little by little, maybe together they could build it up again.

"I'm sorry if I ever hurt you or didn't see you." He sighed and gently squeezed her hand.

She squeezed back and leaned closer until their shoulders touched again. She had spent so much energy holding on to her anger. With that one touch, she finally let go.

"I see you now." His other free hand rose to tuck a stray lock of hair behind her ear.

She caressed the scruff of his cheek with the back of her hand. "I see you, too."

"Can I tell you something?" Mark leaned into her orbit. "Those last few hours stuck in the closet with you were some of the most terrifying and horrible moments of my life."

A hot, fat tear sprung from the corner of her eye and took her by surprise.

Mark caught the tear with the pad of his thumb and wiped it away. "I would do it all over again. I would face a thousand storms if it meant that I could just hold you again."

A laugh exploded from deep inside her as she pulled him near. She threw her head back and laughed again into the impossibly clear night sky.

Mark gazed back from under a heavy brow. "What?"

Melody brushed the tangled hair from his eyes and caressed his cheek. She smiled so wide and true her cheeks ached. "Mark Fox, you don't have to put on a television act."

"I would never." His eyes shone as he smiled

through the dark.

"Then kiss me again." She pulled his face toward hers.

"Melody, I…"

But his words were muffled as she curled her fingers through his hair and pulled him to her until their lips and bodies and hearts collided. Stranded on a lush tropical island of a bedspread in the center of so much wreckage, Melody and Mark found comfort in each others' arms. They tumbled together against the crashing sound of waves under a dark, silent, star-filled night, harboring together once more against another kind of storm.

Chapter Twenty

Mark was hot. Hot, and slick with sweat that stuck the backs of his legs to the bed like glue. Tendrils of dark, damp hair adhered to his neck as the humid, salty air from the beach hovered over him in the open night sky. He should have been uncomfortable, begging for a shower and some decent air-conditioning, but he wasn't. Melody was also sticky and sweaty and glowing with heat at his side. He wasn't miserable; he was in heaven.

Mark stared up at the navy sky, his legs and arms entangled in a maze of soft, luscious limbs and scratchy polyester bedspread. Her mess of fragrant hair was nestled into the crook of his arm as his body continued to hum from the unexpected—yet very welcome—encounter they shared. For the last several hours, he nearly forgot they survived what was likely one of the most intense hurricanes to ever rip through southwest Florida. He didn't care. The smartest, most beautiful meteorologist in the world was by his side.

"You know, you're the first person I've been with since my ex." She sighed.

Her breath caressed his neck as their bodies rose and fell together. "Oh." Mark pursed his lips, unsure how to respond. "Is that…good?"

"Yes." She nuzzled into his neck.

"Good." Mark turned his attention to the sky. They

spent hours together on that bed, talking and kissing. Losing themselves in each other to forget the horrific reality around them. In a way, it was sort of romantic holding her under an open sky, so exposed and yet so utterly alone. She drifted in and out of sleep, beautiful and oblivious to the wreckage all around them. Mark continued to observe the night and the constellations that constantly shifted overhead. The inky black faded to blue, then purple as the stars snuffed out one by one.

Melody's snore hummed lightly in his ear, a sound he never expected to find endearing. As the purple sky shifted into shades of lilac and rose smattered with puffy white clouds, Mark came to the realization he needed to wake her.

But before dawn, Melody sat up straight in bed and sucked in a deep, ragged breath. She clutched the bedspread around her body and scanned the room as she regained her bearings.

Mark sat up. "Hey, it's okay." He held her head to his chest. "You're with me. The storm is over."

"Oh no." She moaned. "It wasn't just a dream."

"Help should be here soon." He brushed the hair from her eyes. "The sun is almost up."

"Everything okay over there?" Jade's voice rang out through the wee morning hours, followed by a collective peal of laughter that could only come from Ty.

"We're fine. How are you guys?" Mark shouted.

"Oh, we're good." Ty snickered. "You two sound like you're doing *real* good."

"Oh *no*." Melody buried her face into a pillow, her voice a low muffled groan. "They heard us."

"So what?" Mark's ears burned.

"This is *so embarrassing,*" she whispered.

"Hey, Jade," Mark shouted. "Our phones are almost dead. Have you heard anything?"

"Yeah! I just got a text. A rescue team is on the way," Jade shouted.

"We're saved." Melody popped her head up again. "I need to find my shoes."

"Better make sure you're decent." Ty cackled at his own joke.

The heat in Mark's ears spread to the apples of his cheeks. He rubbed his tired eyes and ran a hand over his face and realized that his grown-in scruff was longer and fuller than since his last vacation. As he rummaged through the sheets and located his flip-flops, Mark decided he didn't ever want to have to shave or wear a button-down shirt or tie again.

Mark appreciated her silhouette in the dawning light as streaks of brilliant orange and blood red creased the sky. While he was anxious to get a shower and something to eat, Mark knew he wasn't ready to leave the Mali Kai and go back to Tampa. He wasn't ready to leave Melody.

By the time they were both alert and awake, the sky overhead was already turning from orange to a bright cerulean blue. Cottony clouds populated overhead once again as seagulls soared and squawked their mocking, laugh-like cries. The shoreline receded back almost to its original position, yet a quick peek over the balcony through the shattered glass sliding door showed the hotel was still at least one to two feet underwater somehow.

"We're either going to have to swim out of here or get rescued by the Coast Guard," Mark quipped.

"My phone is officially dead." Melody bit her thumb. "I just wish I could talk to my family and know they are okay."

"I'm sure you could use Ty's or Jade's phone once help comes. Or Russel's."

"Jeeze." She sighed and blew a strand of hair from her face. "I can't even believe this."

"Me, neither." Mark gazed at her shoulder and brushed her hair aside. He wanted to close his eyes and relax into her touch, but there wasn't any more time for that. They needed to get out.

"The Mali Kai is really gone." Melody frowned. "There must be so much damage. I really wish we could do something. We're just trapped here."

Mark considered the situation for a moment, then called out over the roofless top of the hotel. "Hey, Jade. Do we still have any juice in our camera?"

"Yeah," she shouted. "Angela wants to know if we can go live as soon as we get to safety."

"What about you, Ty?" Melody called.

"Nope. WINK's Fort Myers Beach crew is officially done with Hurricane Lorraine coverage."

Melody's shoulders fell.

Mark got an idea. "Hey." He laced his fingers through hers. "I have a proposition."

A loud crash sounded through the hallway outside like a bulldozer or a monster of some kind ripping through the walls.

Melody grabbed hold of Mark's arm.

He struggled to decipher what kind of disaster could possibly be happening now. After a few loud thuds and grunts, Mark recognized the sound of the creature that was coming at them and chuckled under

156

his breath. He rose from the bed and limped to the door on his twisted ankle.

"Mark, don't," Melody said.

"It's okay. It's just Russ." Mark opened the door to the Mali Kai security guard as his massive frame filled the doorway of room 204. Whether through sheer adrenaline or pure brute force, he shifted the massive beam that blocked the hallway and was able to carve a path from Melody's room to the main stairwell.

Russ leaned over and picked something up from the ground and smiled. "Ha!" He popped the top of a tall silver can. "Found one of my beers."

****

Mark was exhausted, rattled, and in pain, but he was grateful to be alive. That morning before seven a.m., all five surviving inhabitants of the Mali Kai resort ventured out from the second floor to meet up with rescue crews below. According to the Bay News 9 producer, a volunteer airboat captain would meet them in front of the hotel and steer them to safety. All they needed to do was to make it out of the crumbling Mali Kai resort safely.

"Watch your step." Russ downed the last of his miracle beer as they wandered through the wreckage.

Mark followed. "Russ, how do we know the power main is off?"

"Well." Russel burped. "I don't think we do. I can assume that the power is out all along the beach, but you never know. There might be a live wire somewhere."

"So, we shouldn't go trudging through the flooded hallway?" Melody pursed her lips.

Mark paused for a moment. "Russ, didn't the hotel

have paddleboards in the gift shop?"

"Yep. Don't know how we'll get to them, though."

"I can go get it," Mark offered.

"How?" Melody frowned. "It's not safe."

"Didn't you ever play 'The Floor is Lava' as a kid?" Mark sized up the hotel lobby. The storm windows managed to hold against the hurricane force winds, and though the first floor was still flooded with a foot of standing water, most of the tables and chairs were still intact. With a little bit of imagination and athleticism, someone could hop across the flooded lobby and make it to the gift shop.

"Wait!" Melody grabbed his forearm. "Your foot is still hurt. Let me do it."

"You sure, Mel?" Ty's eyebrows rose. "I can go."

"I got it." She nodded. "Besides, you and Jade have to babysit all of our expensive gear."

"If you say so," Ty said. "I believe in you, babe."

"Really, you don't have to do this." Panic rose in Mark's throat. The idea of Melody getting electrocuted or even hurt filled him with a sense of dread.

"I'm going to figure out how to get us out of here."

In front of Ty and Jade and Russel, Melody leaned in and—to his utter amazement and surprise—kissed him full on the mouth. The feel-good chemicals from the night before came flooding back into his system. His brain was rendered temporarily useless again.

"Be right back."

Mark quit arguing.

Melody kicked off her still-soaked flats and surveyed the area.

Jade nudged him with her elbow and whispered "nice" in his ear.

Melody hopped from the third step on the staircase to a wooden bookcase along the wall. The gift shop and gear rental station were within sight, but instead of a hallway, a river stood in their way.

With the possibility of live wires zapping electricity through the water, the floor literally *was* lava.

After a few well-placed hops and jumps, Melody reached the gift shop and grasped the door frame, then disappeared around the corner.

Mark craned his neck to see where she landed, hoping she made it onto a chair or a counter. After a few moments, an exuberant "a-ha!" echoed from the depths of the gift shop, out of his line of sight.

"What's going on?" Jade craned her neck to get a better look. "Everything okay?"

After a few more moments of silence, a faint splashing sound rippled through the air. Melody emerged from the gift shop, standing atop the paddleboard, maneuvering the board like a pro and glowing like a water goddess. Mark thought over the last few hours that the way he felt about Melody was different, but now as she returned to them, shining with pride and full of power, he knew. He didn't just *like* Melody Orlean. He knew he wanted more than a kiss or a night spent talking under the stars. Whatever was blossoming between them, he wanted it to be something more.

"I think I can manage the paddleboard." Melody lowered to her knees. "But I found something that all of us can use a little easier." She tossed her paddle to Mark and revealed four large, square boxes balanced on the back of the board. "Thought you guys might appreciate these."

A big smile spread across Mark's face as he regarded the inflatable child-sized boat on the package. Each blow-up vessel was small, but just big enough for each of them to be safely floated out of the hotel through the dangerous standing water. They would find a way out of their shared catastrophic nightmare, after all. "Melody Orlean." Mark shook his head and grinned. "I think I'm falling in love with you."

Chapter Twenty-One

Melody blew a gust of hot air into the plastic toy valve, trying hard not to think about the fact that Mark Fox said that he *loved* her. The flooded resort lobby spun as she finished her work, making her already inebriated thoughts even fuzzier. Her head was light as she huffed and puffed into the inflatable boat and simultaneously seethed about a few small, but not so insignificant, words. 'I love you' was a throwaway phrase, after all, and something she said to her own friends all the time. What did it mean to say you loved someone, anyway?

Melody chomped down and tasted plastic again as she blew the realization of what Mark said away. She couldn't let three little words consume her, not with a major task at hand. Not when she still didn't know how her family and the rest of Lee County fared through Hurricane Lorraine.

"Thanks for blowing mine up, Mel." Ty supported her gear as she worked. "I've been feeling a little wheezy. I think that my inhaler got lost in the storm."

"No biggie." Melody forced a smile.

Ty quirked an eyebrow, pursed his lips together, and leaned over. "What is going on?"

Melody shrugged. "I'm blowing up a boat so we can get rescued."

"Don't play all innocent." Ty huffed. "I mean

161

between you and Mr. Sexy Rugged Weather Man over there."

Melody snorted and smiled at Mark. His face was pink from inflating his own boat, nearly the same hue as his neon floral shorts. The shadow of his forehead bruise had almost faded and a nice full growth of stubble filled in around his jawline. The castaway-surfer-guy look suited him. "He said that he *loved* me." She secured the plastic nozzle on the boat and passed it to Ty. "What the heck was that all about?"

"Maybe he does?" Ty shrugged. "You *did* just kiss him in front of all of us."

"How? How can he love me? We don't really know each other." Melody needed to get in contact with her brother. She checked her phone again on muscle memory but remembered the battery was dead. She was trying to stay positive and do what needed to be done to get them all out, but the anxiety building in her chest was getting harder and harder to ignore. She couldn't get home to San Carlos Park fast enough.

"Sounds like you got to know each other enough last night." Ty suppressed a giggle.

Melody gently nudged him with her paddle. "Shut up."

"I'm just saying, you've both been through a traumatic event together." He grinned. "That sort of intense interaction, amplified by some twenty years of romantic tension…"

"Hey. He barely knew I existed twenty years ago. Plus, we didn't exactly get off on the right foot. Now we have one wild hurricane night and he's throwing out the 'L' word."

"Someone telling you they love you isn't the worst

thing in the world, you know," Ty whispered. "Give him the benefit of the doubt, Mel. At least until we're back on dry ground."

"Hold this." She handed him a nylon length of rope. "Wind it through the grommets."

"Fine." Ty eased himself into his inflated kiddie boat, his long legs jutting out in uncomfortable-looking angles. "I just don't want you to throw something away because he maybe got a little excited."

Melody pursed her lips together and frowned.

Mark and Jade descended from the stairs.

Russel was at their heels with his own inflatable boat like some strange kind of fifth wheel.

The idea of the tough guy security guard squeezing his huge frame in the kiddie boat was almost comical. Melody caught Mark's eye and attempted a smile. "Did you film your final segment?"

"No." Mark frowned. "There's no time. We need to get out of here. My producer won't be happy, but we can't waste another moment waiting around."

"We secured all of the gear in the driest closet we could find." Jade huffed. "We'll have to come back for our cameras and stuff later."

"Makes sense." Melody nodded. "Russ, you said there was an emergency door at the end of the hall?"

"Yup." Russel took a swig from a tall, silver can. "Oh, also I found my other beer."

Melody rolled her eyes. "So, we can just push this emergency door open. Even with all this standing water? It seems really unsafe."

Russel shrugged. "It's the best thing I can think of. You can't pry the automatic doors open, so this is our only way out."

"It's worth a try," Mark chimed in and gave her a hopeful look.

Melody assumed her position on the paddleboard again. "I'll lead the way. Ty can hold on to this rope tied to my waist, and I'll pull you all along behind me."

One by one, Ty, Mark, Jade, and Russel eased onto their boats from the stairwell and bobbed in the standing water of the Mali Kai hallway. Ty held onto the rope with one hand and held onto Jade's hand with the other, followed by Mark and Russel in a chain of inflatable boats.

Melody focused on the task at hand, engaged her core, and paddled along the same hallway she walked so many times before during her stay at the Mali Kai. They passed the conference room to the right, which was still also flooded in a foot of water. Fireworks of light sparked in the air from a section of the wall dripping with insulation. Exposed wires and sagging drywall surrounded the live wire in the huge section torn open from the storm. Melody swallowed her fear and was glad for the paddleboard and plastic boats. The farther they traveled down the hall, the darker the corridor became, but she could almost make out a set of double doors at the end. "Almost there." As she approached the heavy, solid doors, Melody realized the plan might not be as foolproof as she hoped.

"Don't touch it, Mel," Ty warned. "The door is metal. You'll get zapped."

"I'll come get it," Russel grumbled.

Melody's paddleboard rocked in the wake of the flooded corridor as Russel wobbled in his kiddie boat from side to side.

"Cut it out, Russ," Mark yelled.

The panic in his voice frightened Melody as she struggled to regain her balance. She was beginning to regret her escape plan. Fear rose in her throat in hot, burning waves.

"Let's think about this." Mark rubbed his temples. "Ty, pull me up. Together maybe we can kick the push bar open."

"That might work." Ty nodded.

Ty, Mark, and Jade worked together to maneuver their floating islands toward the back emergency door. After a few minutes of struggling, the crew was in position.

"My right leg is still pretty good." Mark extended his leg. "I'll kick at the right door, and you kick at the left. Will that work?"

"Worth a try," Ty said. "On three."

Mark nodded. "One. Two. *Three*."

The two men kicked and pushed at the heavy emergency door at the same time with little success.

Ty panted and glanced back at Mark. "Let's try kicking one door at a time."

"Okay. On three again."

The two men worked together while Melody stood back with her heart leaping from her throat. One wrong move and they could be dumped in the possibly electrically charged and dangerous standing water. This time, however, Mark's and Ty's combined kicks forced the door to open halfway as brilliant early morning light spilled into the darkened hall.

"You did it," Jade yelled from behind.

Melody studied Mark's tired, but relieved, face as the sun shone on him. Despite all of the horrors they endured, he was still smiling.

He and Ty exchanged high fives.

That warm, honey feeling spread through her chest again. In that moment, he reminded her of the Mark Fox from college who was everyone's carefree best friend, and something like pride flooded her chest. At that moment, she realized maybe she loved him, too. "Okay." She nudged the door open all the way with the end of her oar. "Let's get the hell out of the Mali Kai."

****

"I'm going to miss that place." Melody looked over at Mark as she sat on the paddleboard across the street from the Mali Kai resort and stared in awe at the destruction left from Hurricane Lorraine.

The crew paddled across the flooded resort parking lot, past the wrecked sign, and through a maze of overturned cars and debris, finally reaching the safety of the elevated median across the street. Almost every resort along the beach within eyesight sustained some type of storm damage, but none were quite so affected as the landmark Polynesian resort. The fact that both news crews escaped unharmed and alive was nothing short of a miracle.

"It was just a hotel." Melody sighed and picked at the now very chipped polish on her nails. "Just a fake, tropical-themed tourist trap that tried to call itself a resort."

"I had some good memories there." The hint of a smile started in the corner of his mouth.

Melody almost smiled, too.

Ty and Jade were at the opposite end of the grass median, surveying the wreckage for themselves and commiserating they wished they were able to film. It was a shame; a group of television journalists stranded right in the middle of a huge weather story with no way to document it. Not that Melody would ever be able to scrub Hurricane Lorraine and the things she witnessed from her mind. "So, you're probably heading back to Tampa pretty soon then?" She worked to keep her poker face intact. "I wonder if the interstate is shut down."

"Possibly. I'm in no hurry. When I return to the station, I'm putting in my notice."

"Really?" Melody's stony expression was in danger of breaking. "Why?"

Mark winced and stretched his legs out in front of him. "It's time to give FoxForecasts a real shot. I think after the storm coverage, I'll have enough followers to monetize my channel now. I'll get some sponsors and do a little more marketing research. I'm done being fake. I want to do what I love and have no regrets."

"You can just do that?" Melody laughed. The words came out a little harsher than she intended.

"I mean, not really." He shrugged. "I have a little bit of cash in savings, but I'm not rich by any means. I'll never know until I try. Heck, if it works, I might need a co-meteorologist."

Melody shifted in her seat. "I don't know."

A loud buzz sounded in the distance like the drone of a million killer bees, breaking the tension in their conversation. Fort Myers Beach was quiet after the storm, with no tourists or traffic to drown out the natural sounds of the sea. The chainsaw-like noise cut through the air like a knife. Melody recognized the source of the mind-rattling drone right away. An airboat.

Melody jumped to her feet and shielded her eyes

against the already glaring, mid-morning sun with her hope refreshed anew. The boat was coming along slow and steady as it navigated through the flooded parking lots and road leading to the resort. As the watercraft drew nearer, Melody identified the captain of their rescue team and gasped. She jumped and clapped as she pulled Mark to his feet. "Austin! It's my brother. We're saved."

Melody brought her hands to her cheeks and let out a sob. Her anxiety over her family's safety swelled and exploded into a burst of tears. Her baby brother was a sight for sore eyes in his backward Tampa Bay baseball cap, sleeveless T-shirt, and reflective lens sunglasses.

Austin snapped his gum between his teeth and grinned as he steered the boat toward then. He cut the engine, killing the buzz saw noise. "You look like you just lived through a hurricane." Austin hopped off the boat and onto the median.

Melody ran to her brother and wrapped her arms around his neck. "Where's Ma? Is she okay?"

"*Hi, Austin, glad to see you're doing okay.*" He rolled his eyes and hugged her back. "Of course, Ma is all right. She's the one who forced me to borrow Mr. Mackey's airboat to come haul your sorry butt outta here."

"Where's Mr. Mackey?" Melody pulled away from their embrace, blinking. "And how do you know how to drive an airboat?"

"I've been training. Mr. Mackey is gonna hire me to work with him on his tours." Austin's eyes darted from Melody to the rest of the crew. "Anyway, Mackey's out with his other boat, searching for more survivors. We need to get going, though, because I'm

168

taking this out to Sanibel next and see if there's anyone stranded."

"Mom's okay then? What about the house?"

"Fine. Everything is good. She's having coffee with Mrs. Mackey and working on a puzzle or something."

"That's amazing." Melody laughed and clasped a hand to her chest. Tears sprung to her eyes, and a little lump settled into her throat.

"So, is this everybody?" Austin shoved his hands into his shorts pockets and surveyed the scene.

"Yes. My cameraman Ty, that's Russel, and Jade." Melody turned to Mark, who stood back as she reunited with her brother. "And this is Mark Fox."

Austin frowned and lowered his sunglasses on the bridge of his nose, his eyes darting from Mark and then back to Melody again. "Wait, isn't this the guy who…"

"Nope!" Melody wiped the wetness from her eyes and shot her little brother the "shut up" stare of death.

Austin's eyes flashed, and his brows scrunched as he pushed his sunglasses up the bridge of his nose and rummaged around underneath the seat of the airboat bench. He brought out five pairs of noise-canceling ear headphones.

"You guys will want to put these on," he said. "It's gonna be a heck of a ride back home."

Home.

The lump grew bigger in Melody's throat as she contemplated the damage her hometown experienced from the storm. Memories of downed power lines, ripped off rooftops, and entire neighborhood blocks flattened to the ground came rushing back. She wasn't ready to face that level of destruction in her hometown once again. She wasn't ready to face the way she was feeling about Mark either. As she slipped the noise-cancelling muffs over her ears, Melody knew that there was no use in running or hiding. When it came to the future, she was going to have to ride out the storm.

Chapter Twenty-Two

Mark's face stung as warm, salty air peppered his face and bare arms. His whole body buzzed as the rescued crew from the Mali Kai coasted back into town and away from flooded Fort Myers Beach, thanks to their unconventional rescue. In all his years living in Florida and working as a meteorologist, Mark never stepped foot on an airboat before, and now with his face permanently plastered to the back of his skull, he was beginning to see why. The fast and noisy ride back to safety didn't put him on edge. The long, tiresome hurricane-filled night didn't make him anxious either. Melody Orlean held his heart in her hand, and by all accounts, she had squashed it.

Melody's chilly reception after their intense weekend left him feeling flat and confused. Their unexpected night spent together—first in the closet and afterward under the stars—awakened something deep within him. Melody inspired him. She reminded him of how far he'd come from the selfish, irresponsible young man he used to be and how he didn't want to backslide into becoming that guy again. She made him laugh. She made him...

Ugh.

Now he was beginning to wonder whether he had imagined the whole thing.

Melody's brother informed them of the state of

things they would be returning to in town. Most of the county was still without power, but only a small section of the highway was closed. A rental van sent from his producer at Bay News 9 was waiting at the WINK News station. Apparently, the producers of both news stations loved the combined hurricane coverage of him and Melody in the closet, after all. Not that Mark cared.

Melody continued to give her brother a rundown of the storm as he, Ty, Russ, and Jade all exited the boat. They reached an area of high ground that wasn't underwater near a fast-food restaurant with half of its sign missing on US 41. As Melody's brother promised, a WINK News van was already there waiting and the exhausted crew filed out of the boat and over to the shuttle van.

Ty gave the van driver a high five and a hug. "Are you coming, Mel?"

Jade and Russel disappeared into the van.

Melody's gaze darted to Ty and then met Mark's gaze.

He searched her expression waiting for…what? He wasn't sure. Closure? Or continuation? Anything, really. They both *had* been through a lot in the last forty-eight hours, and they didn't owe each other anything. But he couldn't part ways with her like this, either.

"I'm staying to help Austin find more survivors. I'll catch up with you later."

Mark sighed and nodded. He gave her a half smile, half frown and extended a hand. "It's been a pleasure. Good luck with everything."

Melody gazed at his hand and winced.

An overwhelming sense of déjà vu overcame him

as he recalled their first professional encounter a few days ago. She didn't accept his reach then, either.

Melody took his hand but didn't shake it as she caressed his cheek with her other hand. Her lips were pursed into a tight frown as she searched his eyes.

For what, he didn't know.

She leaned in and pressed her lips to his.

A dry, rigid kiss—it was a kiss that felt sad and final somehow. It was a kiss that tasted like goodbye.

"Goodbye, Mark. Get home safe." Melody sniffed, turning away in a flash of dark hair and pink, soft curves.

Austin revved the deafening motor of the airboat once more and sped off back onto the wreckage left by Hurricane Lorraine and the maze of flooded beach hotels and condos.

His heart sank as they disappeared into the distance and the woman he loved was gone once more.

****

Mark leaned his forehead against the van window and stared out at the littered highway as they drove toward the WINK News station. He was quiet the entire ride back.

Jade and Ty talked amongst themselves in hushed tones.

Russel, on the other hand, was speaking his mind loud and clear. "What the heck is wrong with you, Fox? That meteorologist was hot for you, man. You just let her leave."

"I did *not*." Mark frowned. "She had to go help her brother."

Russel shook his head and offered a smug frown. "I would never have let go of a lady like that. She's the real deal, and you let her slip away."

"Yeah, man." Jade shrugged and plugged her phone into the van charger. "You blew it."

"Well, what was I supposed to do?" Mark buried his head in his hands. "I came on too strong. Then I didn't come on strong enough. She probably hates me all over again."

"Okay, I can tell you from personal experience that she does *not* hate you." Ty poked his head in between him and Jade. "You can fix this. You said you love her. Now *show* her."

Jade's phone lit up on the charger, signaling it was powered once more. Immediately her phone began ringing in her hand, demanding attention.

Their producer Angela's name shone loud and clear.

"Maybe you should take this one." Jade grimaced and handed over her phone.

He hoped to save this conversation with his producer for when he got back home. After the last few days he endured, he supposed one more face-off wouldn't kill him. He groaned and cradled the phone next to his ear. "Hello, Angela."

"You and Jade missed the 7:00 a.m. feed." His producer's voice was stern on the other line. "What gives?"

"Oh, we're doing fine by the way, thanks for asking." Mark rolled his eyes. "Listen, we didn't have time. We needed to get out of there."

"That's inexcusable," Angela shouted. "First the skimboarding and then that cutesy little feed from your pet project channel," she continued. "So unprofessional. And Jade, she didn't even get any footage of the aftermath, at all…"

Mark could picture her frothing at the mouth on the other line, hunched over in her little studio chair with a fancy coffee at hand. What he was about to say next almost made him wish he was there to see it. "This isn't Jade's fault. We couldn't bring our equipment back. And as for me, you don't have to worry about me being professional anymore. I quit." Mark passed Jade's phone back and smiled as Jade stared, open-mouthed. "It's for you."

"Dang, Fox!" Ty offered his signature high five of approval.

"Hey, my street is the next light." Russel yawned. "Mind dropping me at my place?"

The WINK News van driver nodded and followed Russel's directions to a little suburban neighborhood off the main highway.

As the van pulled up, Mark couldn't help but notice that Russel's modest, trim little home appeared to escape any storm damage, save for a felled palm tree and general debris scattered all around. But the thing that caught Mark's attention more than anything else was the aquatic vehicle parked in his driveway.

"Bye, everybody." Russel rounded up the crew in a series of bear hugs, starting with Jade, Ty, and finally, Mark. "Looks like I'll be looking for a new job. If you know of anywhere looking to hire a security guy, give me a holler."

"Hey, Russ." Mark followed him out of the van. He sucked in a deep breath and scanned the driveway one more time, more certain than ever of what he needed to do. "I was wondering if I could ask you one more favor."

Chapter Twenty-Three

"Why didn't you answer me? I tried to call you like a million times!" Melody wiped the sweat from her brow and scanned the horizon. She shielded her eyes from the near midday sun; her entire body felt sticky with sweat, exhausted, and well on its way to being sunburned. She probably should have gone home to shower and rest like everyone else in the crew, but she was compelled to help her brother search for survivors. She was starting to regret her decision, though. She could be sitting in the air-conditioning relaxing right now. With Mark.

"Sorry." Austin shrugged. "This boat is loud. Plus, Ma was fine, and I was busy chillin' with Mackey's daughter. You remember Chastity, right?"

"*Austin.*" Melody groaned. "I don't want to hear about your hurricane hook-up."

"Well, I wasn't gonna tell you anyway." He gently socked her in the arm. "What about you, though?"

A pang of guilt crept into her chest. "What *about* me?"

"You were texting me complaining about that Mark Fox guy all weekend. Then I showed up, and he looked at you like he was in love or something."

Melody crossed her arms and sank back into her seat. *In love or something.* "We had...a moment. But that was it. Mark lives in Tampa. I'm here."

Austin raised a hand to shield his eyes and scanned the horizon. "Tampa is only two hours away. It's been six months since your divorce, Mel. You're allowed to be happy again, you know."

Melody shook her head and picked her fingernails. Her nail polish was almost completely gone now. "We just got caught up in the moment together. He'll go back to his nice, cozy job in Tampa and forget all about me."

"I don't know. Sounds like you're thinking too much. Like always."

Melody was tired of talking. She was tired of thinking about how poorly things ended with her and Mark Fox. Handsome, good-natured, big-hearted Mark Fox. The same Mark Fox who told her he loved her a little too soon. She wanted her brother to be right. She wanted to give in and throw caution to the wind and to take a chance again. But the idea of someone getting close again was terrifying. Especially since she likely felt the same way toward him, too. It was easier to run, to push away and to hide. Anything was easier than letting Mark Fox break her heart again.

The radio at Austin's hip blipped and crunched out a static signal, indicating he was receiving an incoming message. They floated around, idling the airboat for half an hour with no sight of stranded hurricane survivors. Mr. Mackey was supposed to be calling him soon with the location of a new place to check out.

Austin brought the walkie to his face. "Mackey Marine II, over."

"We got a call saying to check out the Sandpiper, over." The voice of Mr. Mackey crackled through the speaker. "Oh, also, Linda says for you two to come home soon. Over."

"Okay, boss. We'll go take a look out there and then head back in. Over."

"I should have gone back." Melody frowned. "I don't think I can do this anymore."

"Do what? Search and rescue?" Austin scanned the horizon again with his binoculars.

A flock of ibis soared low overhead toward the direction of the ruins of the Mali Kai, creating a V-shaped shadow overhead. A jab of regret hit her in the core that she would never be able to see the inside of the kitschy hotel again. The last place she and Mark were together...their place. "No. I'm done with meteorology. Well, being a news meteorologist, anyway. I tried my best to warn the public, and people still got stuck in this storm."

"You can't quit. You're a natural. You've been practicing to become a weather lady since we were little."

Melody shook her head. "Just talking about the weather isn't doing anyone any good. I need to go deeper. I need to get people to think about how their actions are causing all of this."

Melody and Austin grew quiet as a huge chunk of roofing floated past the airboat. Even though thirty years passed, the terrifying memory of living through Hurricane Andrew still crawled under their skin, the trauma bonding them not only as siblings, but as survivors, forever. But Melody and Austin weren't those two little kids trapped in their bathroom, protected by their mother anymore. Now they were the ones who needed to be strong.

The idea that so many people must have lost their

homes, and possibly even their lives in Hurricane Lorraine, fired Melody up all over again. "You know what? Forget it. If Mark can make a change, then so can I."

Austin cocked his head to the side and placed a hand to his ear, as though listening to something very faint and far away.

Melody heard it, too—a low whine in the distance coming up from behind.

Austin frowned and lifted his binoculars in the direction of the muffled drone, twisting and focusing the lenses to get a better look. "Speaking of." He handed Melody the binoculars with a big, dimpled smile. "I think your man is heading this way."

"What?" Melody snatched the binoculars from her brother. She readjusted the lenses, and her mouth opened wide. Every single thought disappeared as her brain struggled to comprehend what she was seeing. She squinted against the midday sun, and everything became clear. Her senses sprang back to life again, her heart beating fast and furiously in her ears. Warm rays of light sparkled from her chest to her fingertips and toes as she registered the double-vision image through the viewfinder. Like a sunburned knight riding on a white watercraft, Mark Fox was headed her way. "He's back." She lowered the binoculars and then lifted them again. "Why is he back?"

Austin smirked. "Maybe he forgot something at the hotel?"

Melody gave him a swift, sisterly slap on the back of his arm. She couldn't take her gaze off him. The rumble and buzz of the watercraft grew louder as he neared, his swim trunks glowing against his skin. As he closed in on them, Melody realized the man riding toward her transformed over their weekend together. The buttoned-up, snarky meteorologist was gone, and in his place was the man she always wanted to get close to in college. The very same man who was slowing and approaching the airboat at that very moment.

The watercraft came to a slow, gurgling halt. The waves caused the airboat to rock ever so gently in the standing water.

Mark panted and wiped a film of sweat from his brow, all the while never losing Melody's gaze.

They stared at each other for a moment, bobbing on the highway of water and surrounded by the wreckage from Hurricane Lorraine, neither of them moving or able to speak.

"Yo, Mark...what's up?" Austin's gaze darted from Melody and then back to Mark again.

Melody's lungs burned from holding her breath and holding back all the things she wanted to say. Her lips throbbed from too much sun and from being sealed tight. Her head spun from lack of sleep and the rollercoaster of emotions her body endured over the weekend. Mostly, her heart sustained too much damage, and she had no one to blame but herself. She swiped a wisp of sweaty hair from her eyes. "What are you doing here?"

"Thought I would come and see if you needed any help with search and rescue."

"Where'd you get that sweet ride from, man?" Austin shuffled to the side of the boat to ogle at the watercraft. "White and purple. Rad."

"It's Russel's, believe it or not." Mark smiled. "He let me borrow it."

"We'd love some help with search and rescue," Austin said. "We're going back out to the Sandpiper, and then heading in."

Mark bobbed in the water and met Melody's gaze.

She stared back at her hands, unable to hold eye contact. There were so many things she wanted to say. The hard shell she encased her heart in was beginning to crack. "Why are you *really* here, Mark?" Melody glanced up from her worry-ruined nails with eyes full of hope. Love was a throwaway word. Her ex-husband said it plenty of times, but he never really meant it. Love came through showing and doing, and Mark didn't exactly have a great track record with relationships by his own admission. If she was willing to let her guard down and let Mark Fox completely break her heart, she needed to know he was in it for real. She needed to know he would be worth going through that pain all over again.

"I didn't like the way we left things." Mark glanced toward Austin.

Austin leaned against the airboat rails, listening to their conversation intently.

Melody gave Austin a look. "Can we have a minute?"

"Oh." Austin straightened. "I'll just…um. I think I need to go test out those new earmuffs."

Melody smirked.

Austin returned to his captain's chair and placed a set of noise-canceling headphones over his ears.

She propped her hands on her hips and returned her gaze to Mark. The sun was spilling on his hair and shoulders, casting him in a warm, golden glow and exposing coppery red sparkles in his stubble she failed to notice before. Only twelve hours before, they were huddled together in a closet as the sky rained down around them. "You were saying?"

"I think that I might have said something that made you uncomfortable." He ran a hand through his hair.

The tattoo on his bicep caught her attention again.

"I didn't mean to push you away. I wanted to apologize and step back, if that's what you need."

Melody smiled and sucked in a deep breath. "Gloria."

Mark frowned and shook his head. "What?"

"My middle name is Gloria." She laughed. "After my grandmother. She was stubborn, like me."

"Melody Gloria Orlean." His smile returned. "I like it."

"Good. I need you to remember so I won't have a reason to get mad at you some day."

"Gloria. Gloria. Gloria." He leaned on the watercraft handles with his forearms. His smile was as bright as the sun that shone now. "I'll never forget it."

Mark extended a hand her way again in invitation, but this time, not for a business handshake. Melody held onto the airboat rail with one hand and balanced as she accepted his reach. With one foot on the airboat and the other on the floor of the watercraft, Melody swung a leg onto the purple padded seat and planted herself facing backward in Mark's lap.

"Whoa." He steadied the watercraft as best he could as it swayed in the flood. "I don't know if I can drive this thing with you straddling me like this, but I'll gladly give it a try."

Melody still held onto his shoulders as they bobbed along, floating away from the airboat now.

Mark continued to hold onto the handles with one hand, his other placed at her lower back.

"Do you actually know how to drive one of these things?" She lovingly caressed the cut along his eye with the pad of her thumb.

"No." He laughed. "I figured it out, though. I needed to come see you."

"I'm glad you did." The palm of her hand ached for the roughness of his cheek. She closed her eyes and sighed at the texture, at the heat of her skin against his. "I'm sorry, Mark. I'm sorry I ever doubted you."

"Say my name like that again, and I'll forgive you."

Their faces were so close that his breath caressed her lips. "Mark Fox." She curled her arms around his neck. "I think I love you, too."

The last time Melody kissed Mark, she thought it would be goodbye. She thought she would never see him again and that their lives would drift apart. She thought whatever happened between them dissipated— that their time together was brought on by an intense system of emotions that came in unexpectedly to destroy her. Then, like the storm, her romance with Mark would be gone the next day, and she would be left with the mess. She was wrong. Mark wasn't the storm; he was the sun.

They kissed each other among the wreckage, forgetting all about logistics and common sense. They held onto each other, and Melody finally sensed something she didn't expect as she lost herself in his kiss. Her entire being was flooded in a mix of relief and belonging. In his arms, everything would be all right.

"Hey, so… I need to go pick up those folks at the

Sandpiper now," Austin yelled.

Melody held on to Mark's shoulders as they separated, her head spinning as they both looked in the direction of her brother's faraway voice. They had drifted about a hundred feet from the airboat. "Austin! Oh my gosh. Sorry, we'll be right there."

"Don't worry about it. You look busy." Austin snickered. "I'll go take care of this. You guys head back in."

"Are you sure?" Mark held her even tighter around the waist.

"Yeah, something tells me you two need to go take a shower." Austin no longer tried to suppress his laughter. "A cold one."

"I'll meet you back home then, jerk-face." She threw her brother a playful but still obscene gesture. "Love you."

"Love you, too, sis." Austin fired up the obscenely loud airboat and waved goodbye.

Melody held onto Mark, hugged him tight, and closed her eyes. She pressed her face into his back, breathing him in and attempting to seal the moment in her memory forever. The last few days had been full of unreal moments: lightning strikes, floods, harrowing escapes, their night spent together under the stars. But none of them compared to that moment. It was the moment her heart broke from its shell and allowed him in. It was the moment she was able to give him back what he already gave to her. It was the moment she knew she was his, and he was hers, and there was no going back from that moment now.

Melody sat up and wiped a hint of wetness from her eyes.

Mark looked back and smiled, brushing the remnants of her phantom tears. "Are those sad tears?" His forehead creased; the shadow of their twin bruises now almost completely gone.

"No. They're happy tears. I didn't think I would ever see you or speak to you again."

"Did you think I would never talk to my favorite FoxForecasts co-host again?"

Melody gave him a half-smile, half-frown. "Come on, let's get going." She stood and swung her leg around the back of the seat. With a little bit of effort, she switched positions as they bobbed along in the water. She wrapped her arms around his waist and pressed her ear to his back, hot and comforting to the touch and warmed by the sun. "I'd like you to come meet the rest of my family." Melody held on even tighter.

"I'd like that." He revved the engine, making sure to take care of his injured leg. The engine burped, sputtered back to life, and shot forward through the water. "You ready?" Mark gazed over his shoulder.

Melody nodded and held on. Yeah, she was ready. For Mark. For a new beginning. For so much more. The wind whipped past them as they skimmed along the flooded Fort Myers Beach highways and byways toward a future full of hope and love and light.

But first, they would need to return their borrowed watercraft to a muscle-bound security guard named Russel.

Chapter Twenty-Four

"We're here at the site of the Mali Kai resort reconstruction project on the one-year anniversary of Hurricane Lorraine. Melody Orlean relaxed her shoulders with her microphone at hand."As you can see behind me, every hotel on this section of the gulf is still undergoing a massive effort to bring Fort Myers Beach back to where it was before the destruction brought on by the Category 5 hurricane last summer."

Mark held the cue cards and leaned against their Jeep, a wry grin plastered across his face.

Ty stood behind the tripod of their digital camera filming their segment for FoxForecasts as his boyfriend, Luther, looked on.

Jade couldn't make it to their reunion; she was competing in the state disc golf championship but promised to meet up later.

"Florida Governor Wanda Valdez has been working tirelessly with FoxForecasts and the Zero Emissions Initiative. Ms. Valdez, can you tell us what the state is doing to help the Gulf Coast in terms of climate change?"

"Certainly." The statuesque governor spoke into her mic. "We're just now getting the program off the ground. But as you know, this fall we'll have a vote on the ballot to help push tax dollars toward a state-wide green initiative."

"That's amazing." A genuine smile spread across Melody's lips. "Anything else?"

"Yes, as a matter of fact." The governor nodded. "I'm also presenting this same initiative to my fellow Gulf Coast governors in Alabama, Mississippi, Louisiana, and Texas. These powerful hurricanes impact us the most, and we are all committed to changing whatever we can in our home states. It all starts with an ecological curriculum in public schools all the way up to hefty fines for corporations that don't meet our zero emissions standards in the next seven years."

"That's incredible." Melody beamed. "Well, thank you for taking the time to come and speak with us today, Ms. Valdez."

"The pleasure is mine." The governor extended a hand. "We appreciate all that your team is doing to raise awareness for this urgent matter. Global warming affects all American citizens, and not just those in the Gulf Coast."

Melody shook the governor's hand, turned to Mark, and smiled again as the late afternoon sun shone down on their crew. In that moment, she was even more proud than when she became the first generation college graduate in her family. She was even more proud than when she walked away from her bad marriage. She was in the process of making her greatest ambition come true—to help enact real changes that would affect their climate for good and possibly stop so many deadly hurricanes and storms from ravaging the planet for future generations. And she got to do it with the man she loved best of all by her side. "Until next time, this has been Melody Orlean in Lee County with

FoxForecasts, weather *all* the time."

"Aaaand, cut." Ty lowered their digital camera. "That was great."

"Thank you so much, Wanda." Melody shook the governor's hand again. "We'll be in touch."

The governor winked and retreated to where the Lee County mayor was waiting to discuss new flood zone ordinances and evacuation measures.

Melody sighed and glanced at the giant crane that stood still now over the ruins of the Mali Kai. This time last year, she and Mark were holed up in the wreckage of that very building hiding from the costliest storm to ever tear through Lee County. In a stroke of pure luck mixed with hard work, no lives were lost, but all the destruction cost the small Gulf Coast town 18.3 billion dollars in damages.

A familiar sleeveless forearm wound its way around Melody's midsection as she surveyed the damage. She laughed as a brush of scruff kissed her cheek and a fall of soft hair caressed her collarbone. Melody welcomed the embrace with a smile. "Can you believe it's already been a year?" She sighed and turned to face her co-producer, best friend, and partner in life.

"Feels like a lifetime ago." Mark pulled her close.

"Easy, partner." She smiled and wrapped her arms around his neck anyway. "We're professionals, remember? No PDA on the job."

"We're our own bosses." He grinned and angled for a kiss. "We can do what we want."

Melody leaned into him, remembering their first night together on that stormy evening so long ago. Their work led them back to that very spot, surrounded by the friends they cherished and celebrating the work that they both dedicated their lives to. In twelve short months, Melody and Mark threw themselves into a business—and each other—to create an independent weather channel that blended journalism and environmental activism in a way that made them both feel fulfilled.

"Smile, you two," Ty said.

Melody whipped her head around to see Ty and his partner standing side by side. A flash obscured her vision as Ty snapped a photo, causing her to laugh and shake her head. Even in the bright summer sun, his flash took her by surprise. "Ty, we're all done filming." She laughed. "No photos. Please."

She noticed Mark wasn't standing in front of her anymore but kneeling at her feet. "Is your shoe untied or something, babe?" Melody frowned. She should have known better than to ask that, though. Mark Fox only wore sandals these days. She blinked again as she gazed at Mark's impossibly stormy eyes under a swath of devil-may-care hair. The pieces started to come together then. He wore a button-down shirt for the first time in ages that day, albeit a short-sleeved one. He also invested in a nice new pair of twill shorts, and not the kind he would use to skimboard in. Melody assumed Mark dressed up for the governor that day, but as it turned out, he was wearing something nice for a whole different reason.

"Melody Gloria Orlean." Mark gazed at her, still kneeling with one knee propped up.

In his right hand was a telltale black velvet box. Melody received a box like that a long time ago from a man she thought loved her. The idea of ever seeing a box like that again used to scare her and send pins and needles coursing through her veins. But after the year of love and partnership she and Mark shared, the prospect of what might be contained in that little box didn't scare her anymore. Melody's hands flew to her mouth. "Yes?"

Mark opened the box.

She gasped and prickles of adrenaline flooded her veins. A delicate, lilac-colored stone surrounded by round pavé diamonds set on a simple white gold band nestled in the cushions. The ring was an amethyst set in white gold—not flashy and over-the-top like the one she used to have.

"Melody." He cleared his throat. "Will you marry me?"

Melody accepted the box and examined the ring up close. It could have been any ring, and she would have been happy. She plucked the band from its secure presentation and examined it. It slipped onto her finger as if it were made just for her. He even got the size right.

Mark squinted under furrowed brows. "Is that a yes?"

Melody nodded, too overcome to speak as he rose and embraced her, letting her answer him with another deep kiss. More flashes of light happened, and then a wave of applause pulled them apart. They were not enjoying a private moment. They had an audience.

"Surprise!" Ty flashed them again. "Congratulations."

Melody held her left hand, complete with new jewelry to her chest, and surveyed the scene that gathered around them.

Jade made it to the celebration, after all, still

dressed in her disc golf uniform, but present, nonetheless.

Russel wrapped a meaty arm around his new wife, Thalia, and sounded a loud wolf whistle into the air.

Her brother and mother stood off to the side, clapping and rubbing elbows with Mark's parents.

Beyond the familiar faces were dozens and dozens of other faces she didn't recognize but came to wish them well just the same. "Who are all of these people?" Melody whispered.

Mark embraced her from behind. "Your fans. Well, our fans, I guess. They all love you the most though."

Melody choked back a sob and waved as the crowd dispersed, still buzzing from the surprise engagement. To say that having all the people she loved the most here to witness the event was overwhelming was an understatement. Melody Orlean didn't *cry*… but on that day, she did.

"Congratulations!" Linda Orlean dabbed her eyes. She had also dressed for the occasion in one of her signature tropical print dresses, her silver-streaked tresses pinned up in a stylish chignon.

Melody embraced her mother, breathing in her perfume. "Thanks, Ma."

"Where's my new favorite son, huh?" Linda abandoned Melody to embrace Mark in a huge, motherly hug. Linda and Mark had become fast friends over the past year.

"Great, now Ma is *really* going to like Mark better than me." Austin greeted her with a hug. "Congrats, sis."

"Thanks." Melody rolled her eyes. "Maybe you and Chastity Mackey will be next."

"No way." Austin laughed. "I'm never getting married."

She gave him a playful shove. "We'll see about that."

"Hi, Mr. and Mrs. Fox! I'm so glad you could make it." Melody embraced her future in-laws and made the rounds greeting old and new friends alike in the shadow of the ruins of the Mali Kai hotel. Most people probably wouldn't have guessed a construction site would make for a romantic engagement location, but for Melody and Mark, it was meaningful.

As the crowd dispersed, Melody still reeled, winding the ring around her finger. She laughed to herself as friends waved goodbye, promising to meet up at the Bubble Room to celebrate. In a way, she wished she could go back in time and have a good laugh with her twenty-two-year-old self to tell a young Melody to keep pushing and that someday everything would work out.

The last of their friends and family took off toward the landmark Sanibel Island restaurant, leaving Melody and her fiancé alone for the first time. She wasn't ready to leave just yet. She wanted him to herself, to savor the moment just a little while longer. "So, what now, Mr. Fox?" Melody took his hand in hers and tugged him toward the beach. The sun was beginning to dip into the Gulf of Mexico, offering up a dazzling watercolor display. The idyllic coastal view was a sight people traveled thousands of miles to experience, and right then, it was all theirs.

"Well, I guess now we plan a wedding and a honeymoon." He wound his arms around her waist. "We could just elope and go straight to the honeymoon part, too, if you want."

Melody leaned in and kissed him again, slow and sweet and steady. "I think that sounds like a fabulous idea."

"Thank you." He pressed his forehead to hers.

She laughed a little, remembering the first time their foreheads met in a much rougher, less romantic way. "For what?" Melody gazed into his eyes. She still couldn't get over their color and how they matched the churning, salty sea.

"For loving me."

"Loving you is the easy part." Melody squeezed his hand. "Thank you for loving me back."

Mark kissed her on the top of the head as the sun continued to dip lower into the sea.

Melody bit her lower lip. She and Mark never kept secrets from each other, but she had been saving one big secret for the right moment. The secret was a life-changing piece of breaking news for the both of them—news she hoped that he would be excited about too. "There's another hurricane brewing, you know."

"Really?" He glanced at her; his eyebrow knitted together. "I didn't see anything on the Doppler."

"Mmm, no. I don't think anyone knows about this one yet." Melody's eyes sparkled. "I think they'll probably call this one Hurricane Mark."

"Ha ha." He smirked and rolled his eyes. "Mark isn't on the list of storm names this season."

"No?" She offered a soft, warm smile. "What about Hurricane Mark Jr.?"

Mark frowned and shook his head. "I don't get it."

Melody's face fell, and she glared with one eyebrow arched. "*Mark*. I'm *pregnant*."

193

"Oh." Mark's gaze darted back and forth and then grew wide. "Oh!" He wrapped her in a hug and peppered her face with kisses. "I'm so dense. A baby?"

"It's okay, I still love you." She laughed. "Yes. A baby."

"I love you, too."

Melody and Mark held each other as the sun set on Fort Myers beach that day, neither of them sure of what was on the horizon. A hurricane brought them together and nearly tore them apart, and there were likely more storms in their future to navigate through. They would survive all the bad days together with friendship and compassion. They would weather the storms of life, knowing the sun would always shine as long as they had love and each other.

A word about the author…

Wendy Dalrymple crafts highly consumable, short and sweet romances inspired by everyday people. When she's not writing happily-ever-afters, you can find her camping with her family, painting (bad) wall art, and trying to grow as many pineapples as possible.

Keep up with Wendy at
http://www.wendydalrymple.com